My Story

PRINCESS OF EGYPT

Vince Cross

SCHOLASTIC

While the events described and some of the characters in this
book may be based on actual historical events and real people,
this story is a work of fiction.

Scholastic Children's Books
Euston House, 24 Eversholt Street,
London, NW1 1DB, UK
A division of Scholastic Ltd
London ~ New York ~ Toronto ~ Sydney ~ Auckland
Mexico City ~ New Delhi ~ Hong Kong

First published in the UK by Scholastic Ltd, 2008

ISBN 978 1407 10309 9

Printed in the UK by CPI Bookmarque, Croydon, CR0 4TD

2 4 6 8 10 9 7 5 3

Prologue

Egypt circa 1490 BC

Perhaps Senenmut's right. Maybe sometimes I *am* just a stupid, headstrong little girl. I'll admit it, I scared myself badly yesterday. What if I'd broken a leg making that jump, rather than just spraining an ankle? Hulking great soldiers in my father's palace guard have died from as much. One week a "crusher of nations" the next a corpse on the embalmer's slab. There's not much you can do to mend a broken leg. In our climate, infection sets in fast.

It's an uncomfortable thought. I don't want to die. Not yet. At thirteen summers old, I've hardly started.

But then what none of the men in the court of my father, King Thutmose, remotely understand is how boring life can be in the harem. Even dear Senenmut, my tutor. They think all women are the same. They think we just love to sit around each and every day, feeling protected, while *they* strut around looking powerful, having "important conversations". Well not me. I watch some of those girls, plucking their lovely eyebrows, smoothing their shapely legs, rubbing lily-scented ointment into their perfect skin, and wonder what's going on inside their heads. Answer – not a lot! Lamps lit but no one at home, I reckon.

Me on the other hand – I like *doing*. The more active I am, the better my brain works. When I've been running, I just feel so alive. "Don't you ever get tired?" the girls ask. Or (with a faint look of disgust) "How can you stand getting so sweaty?" Or that old favourite (me doing press-ups by the garden pool), "You'll never get a man if you keep doing that, Asha! No one wants a woman with muscles!" I was probably about six when I first heard that one. Well, actually no, I don't get tired. I have *more* energy after a run. Great big wonderful ideas spiral around me. I can feel my *ka* leaping and bouncing for joy. In that moment I think I was born to change the world. I can even pretend I understand Senenmut's arithmetic classes. And I *like* the feeling of sweat trickling down my back, the tingling in my body when I drive myself to the limits of speed and endurance. Any man who wants me will just have to love me for who I am. *"I promise before Amun I will cherish thee, Runner Girl…"* Runner Girl! It's what the other girls call me. As nicknames go, it's not the worst, is it?

But yes, I'll have to think more carefully from now on. *Obviously* roof-running is dangerous – that's partly why I like it – but maybe I've become overconfident. Nofret, daughter of Mutnofret, may be my best friend as well as my half-sister, but I hadn't listened to her. When we'd walked the course the previous day, she'd spotted what I was choosing to ignore.

2

"Are you *really* sure about that jump, Asha? Looks a bit of a stretch to me."

I'd been peeved she'd questioned my judgement. "No problem!" I'd answered, brushing her away, "I can take *that* any day. Watch me go!"

So yesterday at dusk, we'd sauntered past the guards to our chosen starting point, the highest roof of the harem, three storeys up, by the Queen's Tower. It was a perfect evening. A magnificent blood-red sun was sinking behind the cliffs of the western desert. On the far side of the River Nile, the narrow valleys where the royal ancestors rest were deep-cut black scars against the pink ribs of rock. In the nearer distance delicate billows of grey-white mist drifted up slowly from the sacred river as fishermen, washerwomen, boatmen and traders all desperately tried to cram two hours' work into the last hour before sunset. Around us, beyond the harem and the vast palace complex, sprawled the countless grey mud-brick houses which make up the great city of Thebes, capital of the Two Kingdoms of Egypt, the place where every Egyptian dreams of living. This, *all this* and so much more, is the world he rules: the great Pharaoh, son of the sun god Re, Thutmose, peace and prosperity be on him for ever. My dad.

"Have you ever thought," said Nofret, "how strange it all is?"

"What do you mean?"

"We could have been born anywhere. You or I could have been a slave girl. Or a peasant woman, grinding corn all day. Not the daughters of a king."

And for a moment we paused to take in that extraordinary piece of good fortune.

The very end of the afternoon is the best time of day for roof-running, while there's still just enough good light, before Thebes' citizens come up to eat, talk and hold hands in the night air away from the heat and stink which builds up down below among the houses. As I unwound the linen shawls from my upper body, swapping the long sheath of my day dress for a running skirt, the gentlest of breezes began to waft across the rooftops from the north. It brought with it the faint aromas of baking bread and cooking food.

"Ready then?" I said, stretching and twisting. (Here's a tip for you. *Always warm up before you exercise!*) Nofret nodded. She's such a loyal companion, my older sister. We may have different mothers, and we don't look anything like each other (me lanky and plain, she small and pretty), but we think like twins. She doesn't want to run, she's always made that quite clear, but she's never once mocked my favourite pastime. And she's never hinted slyly to anyone that I'll "grow out of it in time". That's a line she leaves to my mother, Ahmose, the King's Great Wife, chief woman of the harem.

"Don't lose count, will you?" I added. As if.

"Just take care of yourself, Asha," she said. "You worry about the jumps. Let me worry about the counting. On your marks … get set … go!"

And I was away, bounding down over the harem roofs. The first hundred paces would be the last hundred paces of my return. Then I curved away down towards the harem gatehouse, leaping over it and out into the suburbs by way of the shops outside the gate, still way above ground level. The smell of bread was at its strongest just there, the odour fading in my nostrils as I leapt from the roof of the last shop on to the houses beyond.

Why should I do such a daft thing? Well, haven't you ever looked at the birds of the air and wished you could be like them? Roof-running's the closest you can get. When I'm up there, I'm free and fully alive, every sense finely tuned, a thrill running through the whole length of my body. But don't *you* go trying it, not unless you have the kind of protection the goddess Hathor and the mother of the gods Nut give me.

Of course, part of the fun's doing something I'm not supposed to. There's no rule that says I shouldn't be outside the harem on my own – the guards aren't there to keep us in, more to keep unwanted people out – but yes, I understand full well people could think it's *unseemly* for a princess, even a thirteen-year-old princess, to jump around the way I do. Especially without telling someone in authority where I'm going and what I'm doing. But what harm is there in it? Let's be honest, to any ordinary Theban I meet while I'm sky-skimming, I'm simply another anonymous, annoying street kid. I'm away and gone far too quickly for them to guess who I am.

Over the houses, I was running parallel to a dirty, manure-filled street. How can people live in such filth? At least up on the roofs there are no animals to trip over, and so, unlike down at street level, there's no dung to leave my legs splattered and smelly. The narrow passageway below me meandered left and right for maybe 200 paces. I twisted and turned with it, leaping the short gaps between the houses every fifteen strides or so. Occasionally a face peered inquisitively at me from a stairwell, and I shot them a reassuring friendly smile. No, I wasn't there to steal their family heirlooms!

At the end of the houses were some stables. I comfortably made the longish jump across the space just there, pulling myself over a parapet wall, legs and bottom slithering and flailing over the mud-brick. No marks for style, but an interesting view for anyone down below! On the far side was another similar wall. I vaulted it fluently and began the flat-out run to the jump Nofret had worried about. The blood was pumping now. In that moment I believed anything and everything was possible. Silly Asha! Over-confidence is such a dangerous thing. I drove my legs full tilt at the leap across the chasm, not giving a thought to the drop, but as I pushed off into mid-air the mud-brick underneath my leading foot crumbled. In that instant, knowing I'd misjudged the jump badly, that Nofret had been right and I'd been wrong, perhaps for the first time in my life I felt fear. Truthfully, the thought of serious injury or death had never occurred to me until then. Now for a terrifying split-second I thought I was going to crash to the paved yard beneath and break my neck. In despair I lunged for the edge of the roof, and the goddess Hathor, praise her name, must have been watching over me because as I fell my stretching hands miraculously found a hold. My feet scrabbled at the mud-brick wall, my whole body jolted and shuddered, but somehow I clung on, and then slowly, painfully, was able to haul myself up on to the roof, safe and more or less in one piece.

I sat there for a while collecting myself, shaking from the shock, looking dumbly at my bruised and bleeding knees. I could just imagine the tutting of the harem girls. "*Oh, look at silly little Asha! When will that girl ever grow up?*" Feeling a complete idiot was bad enough, but then the agony in my ankle kicked in, and I realized what carelessness can cost.

When I tried to stand, my right leg wouldn't bear any weight at all. I clung to a wall for support, and waited miserably for Nofret, knowing I'd have to eat humble pie when she eventually found me.

Which she did, of course. She knew roughly how long the run should have taken – a count of about a thousand was what we'd guessed. When I didn't arrive she fluttered her eyelashes at Senbi the nice young harem guard to come and help her look for me. He didn't need much encouragement to spend a little time close to pretty Princess Nofret!

"Oh, you poor thing," she said, when they finally spotted me leaning against a chimney, trying my hardest to be a brave Pharaoh's daughter and not cry, "You gave me a real fright. I thought someone might have kidnapped you. Whatever would I have said to Father if a ransom note had arrived at the harem?" Leaning on their shoulders, I hopped home feeling very small and stupid.

Enlisting Senbi's help was good and bad. I couldn't have staggered back without him. But questions were quickly asked about why he wasn't where he should have been and then he had to confess to his boss that, sorry, sir, he'd been AWOL rescuing the Princess Hatshepsut, and then Senbi's boss blabbed to my tutor, Senenmut, and so this morning there I was explaining myself to a committee comprising my mum, a stern-looking Senenmut and Inet, my nurse, equally severe. It wasn't a happy interview.

So there you have it. I'm gated, watching the harem girls on their hopeless quest for ultimate beauty until my ankle heals. But as I said, running makes Big Ideas happen. And trust me, after yesterday, I've got a really good one brewing.

Because of course my Big Idea is … yes … you've got it … the papyrus you're holding in your hand now. Treat it very, very carefully! There's been nothing like it, not in the 1,500 years since the great warrior and first Pharaoh Narmer joined up the two kingdoms of Egypt. True, the walls of the temples are covered in writing and our libraries are full of miles and miles of fading documents. But most of that boring stuff was scrawled by old men desperate to leave something behind before they died and made their final journey out to the stars. Believe me, nowhere is there a story like the one I'm going to write. A true story. An exciting story. Well, it's bound to be. It will, after all, be the tale of a Pharaoh's daughter. Look after it well, whoever you are. Maybe it will bring you luck! Maybe my *ka* will live again through you.

So, to begin at the very beginning, let me tell you exactly who I am.

My name's Asha – you know that already. But the common people of Egypt know me by my official royal name – Hatshepsut, only daughter of King Thutmose by Ahmose his Chief Wife, Queen of Egypt. My name means "First among noble women", and maybe one day I *will* be truly noble. But inside my head and to those who love me best, I prefer to be simply Asha.

Soon the star Sirius will rise in the sky, which means that tomorrow the five days' celebration of the New Year begins. As my New Year token, I promise that from now on I'll write down truthfully whatever happens to me during the coming months and years – the good *and* the bad – the time in which my mother Ahmose keeps assuring me her daughter will stop being a silly girl and magically turn into an accomplished, mature woman. As if, by gaining a few feminine curves, she thinks I'll lose my "inclination to foolishness" (i.e. the roof-running!) and become sweet, obedient and interested in weaving. Dream on, Mum. Pigs might fly!

Senenmut smiles indulgently on me and encourages me to write – it's his job – but if my father were ever to find these ramblings, he'd probably tell me to burn them at once. And no doubt Shushu the vizier, the man I call "the vulture", the man closest to the King's ear, would agree with him. Which is exactly what I'd expect of such an unpleasant man. "Women are all very well. In their place!" I've heard him say more than once. Which doesn't stop his liking for vain, glossy harem girls. Especially Esho. I've seen the way they look at each other. Ugh!

But I'll outwit Shushu and the others who want to keep women under their thumb. Doesn't *my* story deserve to be heard as much as any man's? Since in Egypt women can buy land and have a house built, or trade jewellery and corn, shouldn't their lives and opinions matter as much as men's? Go on, let's think the unthinkable. Couldn't a woman one day even become Pharaoh and rule as wisely as any male? Would it so disturb the great god Amun and the *maat* of Egypt?

Maybe that's a word which means nothing to you. *Maat.* It's what our royal family and court exist for. To protect Egypt, and by everything we do to achieve harmony and well-being for our people. It's a sacred duty. And a pain in the neck. We royals may have wonderful palaces in which to live, the best food and clothes, all we could ever want, but we live daily in the knowledge that if we get it wrong and anger Amun, he may punish us and all Egypt with us. And it would be our fault. *My* fault! Imagine carrying *that* responsibility around with you every day.

When I've finished a year's scribbling, my papyri can conveniently disappear into some safe hole in the ground. Then perhaps when I'm an old woman, I'll go and dig them out, and amuse myself reading about me when I was thirteen, before burying them again for you. But first things first. How am I going to manage tomorrow, hobbling up to the temple of Amun for the New Year festival? I'll have to get there somehow, even if Nofret and Senbi carry me. It's something I wouldn't miss for the world.

Book one
FLOOD

Five months later

Well, so much for that New Year resolution. Nearly half a year gone and nothing written. Where should I begin in telling you about the last few months? I *have* changed since last I wrote, I know I have, but definitely not in the way my mother Ahmose hoped for. Maybe life is never what you think it's going to be.

I made it to the New Year festival, leaning on the smooth, polished crutch made for me by a harem carpenter on Senenmut's instructions – his peace offering for being so po-faced about my little adventure. But I didn't enjoy the New Year as I thought I would. It ought to have been a time of celebration, with laughing people filling the streets of Thebes, happy that the granaries were safely full of corn and prosperity was assured. But this year was different. Everyone's mood was dark and dismal. It was hard to raise a smile anywhere. My father spent all his time muttering in corners with the vizier Shushu, and scarcely had a word for me. My brother Wadjmose was busy acting the part of a real adult, so condescending: "You're just a girl, Asha. You wouldn't understand. It's for us men to deal with. Haven't you got enough to keep you occupied? Go and get your hair done. Nofret is *so* much prettier than you! Strange! You'd never think she and Edjmet were related, would you?"

Edjmet is Nofret's brother and he's ugly and stupid, Wadjmose and I agree on that. But my brother can just be so horrible sometimes. I hate him.

Because actually I think I understand very well. For Egyptians the River Nile is everything. Each year, just when the heat is at its worst, and the farmers are exhausted from the efforts of the harvest, at the insistence of the Nile-god Hapi, the tears of the great creator god Amun fill the river and the fields flood. For three, maybe four months, no work can be done there. The farmers mend their tools. They build and repair their storehouses. They conserve water. And they wait. Wait for their yearly presents from Hapi and Amun.

What they hope will be sent to them is rich, black soil washed down from the mountains far upstream, and precious moisture to make the plants grow in that soil. If the floods fail, if the serpent sound of water is slow to rush into the channels the farmers have patiently cut, the harvests will be poor and the people will starve. And for three years now, the waters have been thin and reluctant. Amun simply hasn't been shedding enough tears to grow our crops. However much we've pleaded there's been no reply. The

Pharaoh's repeated sacrifices have been to no avail. These past few months the situation finally became critical. The granaries were nearly empty. The people were beginning to despair, and in some cases becoming rebellious. During the two months after that miserable New Year right up to the festival of Opet, you could feel the tension rising around the city.

"Why doesn't Amun hear us?" I asked Senenmut, as we sat together in the harem schoolroom the day before Opet. "He cares about Thebes, doesn't he? Why doesn't he *do* something?"

"Perhaps he's angry…" Senenmut answered. He seemed distracted, studying something terribly interesting on the far wall. Well, it was a hard question. "…Perhaps somehow we've disturbed *maat*."

"Well, how?" I challenged him. "I don't think you believe that. *Do* you?"

"I don't know. Maybe I do," he said, turning to look at me, stroking his chin thoughtfully. "Can you think of a better explanation why previously the rains were more plentiful in the mountains of the south?"

"Maybe the weather just changes year to year?"

"Yes, but you still have to ask why. It's no good saying something *just* happens, Asha. Push that brain of yours. You're a bright girl. Always look for the reason."

"So what is it we've done that could be so wrong?"

15

Senenmut's brow furrowed. He was treading carefully, avoiding saying what he really thought, it seemed to me.

"Perhaps Egypt isn't the way he wants it to be. Perhaps the people have acted disrespectfully. Or perhaps decisions have been made which have displeased Amun…"

"You mean by my father … decisions made by the King?"

Senenmut looked at me sharply – as if I'd been setting him a trap.

"I didn't say that, Asha. Don't put words into my mouth. Your father is the god's son. You know that. And a great man. How could he displease his heavenly father Amun?"

"Sons *do* fall out with their fathers…"

Senenmut paused, and studied me, as if he was working out how grown-up I was – how much he could take me into his confidence.

"Yes, but not in this case, trust me. Your father Thutmose has been a great Pharaoh for Egypt over the years, and you mustn't ever think differently. But look, Asha, one day you'll have influence. Who knows, you may even become Queen, by the grace of the goddess Hathor. We who are close to the Pharaoh should always remember that any advice offered should be … well considered…"

"You mean Shushu? That *he's* the problem? You *do*, don't you!"

Senenmut looked me directly in the eye.

"An important man. An influential man. None more so.

16

But Asha, you never heard such a suggestion from me. Now, let's get back to astronomy, shall we, and forget matters that don't concern us?"

He meant, of course, matters which didn't concern *me*. Prejudice. That girl/woman thing again. Even from Senenmut.

Intriguing, though. I'd never imagined he and Shushu would get on well together, but this was the best evidence I'd seen yet that they really didn't.

Unexpectedly the Beautiful Feast of the Opet turned out to be everything that the New Year *hadn't* been. It was as though everyone from the humblest servant right up to the King himself were making one last gigantic effort to persuade Amun and Hapi that Egypt's *maat* was in perfect balance and that we deserved a flood and a harvest to make up for the years of drought and famine. And something so astonishing happened to me that even now I'm still trying to take it in.

As the heat of the day dropped from its peak, everyone in the harem, the women, the older children and the servants, got dressed in their finest linen gowns and jewellery, and walked out through streets thronged with cheering crowds to the Temple of Amun at Karnak in the northern part of the city. In front of us and behind marched the harem guards, armed with clubs and spears in case the crowds became too excited. It was a first for me and Nofret. We'd never been allowed to take part in the Opet procession before.

"Don't you just love it?" she shouted over the hubbub. "Isn't this fantastic?"

"Amazing!" I yelled back and meant it. The low sun dazzled us, raucous trumpets and rolling drums assaulted our ears and from every side shouts of "Long live the Pharaoh!" and "Praise to Amun!" echoed from the buildings. We smiled and waved and accepted the adoration of the bystanders. We were on show – the very centre of attention. It was hard to believe, but people were craning their necks just for a glimpse of *us*. Fathers hoisted children on to their shoulders as we passed by.

In less than an hour of joyful mayhem, we were away from the bustle, standing within the private courtyards at Karnak, the street noise still echoing in the distance, waiting in the shade of the temple's mighty columns, watching as the high priests slowly and respectfully mounted the long ramp towards Amun's sanctuary, the place where for most of the year the great god himself lives.

"What exactly do they do in there?" I'd once asked Senenmut when I'd been very small.

"They do for Amun what you'd do for your best friend," he'd answered. "They wake him, feed him, bathe him, dress him in his finest clothes, and bring him the presents he'd like most in the whole world. So then he'll be in the happiest mood to greet the Pharaoh, won't he? Or at least, that's what I *think* goes on, little Asha…"

Because of course, Senenmut had never been inside the sanctuary. Only the high priests go there. And they don't talk about it.

As the sun began to set, a gleaming carriage emerged into the open air from the entrance of the temple, the gold leaf on its surfaces glinting fierily in the low rays. The carriage was set on poles hoisted on the shoulders of temple priests who this one special year in their lives had been granted the honour of carrying Amun the length of the city to meet my father Thutmose in the temple of Luxor at Thebes' southern end. The gorgeous carriage passed by us, no more than twenty paces from where we stood, before we turned and followed it in yet another procession, more solemnly now, back down the avenue of the Sphinx to Luxor. It was slow progress. Although the people made a pathway for almighty Amun, the procession ground to a halt every now and then while someone from the crowd stepped forward to seek guidance from him.

"My brother stole land from me. Is it right that he should receive a pardon?" I heard one man ask from bended knee.

The carriage dipped backwards where it stood. Caught off balance, the guards carrying it swayed and almost buckled at the knees. The answer from the god Amun was "no". He agreed with the questioner's hurt feelings. A scribe made a note of Amun's ruling on a piece of papyrus.

"Can my father disinherit me just because I married a woman he doesn't like?" asked another man.

The carriage dipped forwards and there was a disturbance among the crowd. To their surprise, the answer was "yes". Amun had ruled that the man *could* be disinherited. The man looked angry. But Amun had made his decision, and there could be no appeal.

Maybe as many as fifteen times the carriage stopped to answer similar petitions, but eventually, with the daylight almost gone, we arrived at the southern temple. In the distance we could see my father, lit dramatically by torches set in the tops of the walls, elegant and imperial, his face framed by the twin cobras of his crown, standing high above the crowd to welcome his heavenly father Amun. The priests burst into song, and a ring of dark-skinned Nubians began their stately dance around the carriage and the King as they disappeared out of sight into the temple's dark recesses.

"And what do they do in *there*?" I'd begged Senenmut that time long ago.

"They pray for fruitful planting and an abundant harvest!"

And this year for water. For a full River Nile. How they should be praying for that!

We were ushered off to one side, into an antechamber

next to the holy place where my father was now communing with Amun. High up on one wall was an opening covered with a long reed mat. The temple ushers directed us to make a semicircle in front of it. Shushu stepped forward and bowed to the opening.

"Amun can hear us," Nofret whispered.

I pulled a face.

"No, really, he can," she insisted. "Inet told me. If we ask questions he'll answer."

"Not likely," I whispered back.

"Well no, not you or me. But *they* can. People like Shushu…"

Senenmut glared at us, Inet squeezed my arm, and we took the hint, falling silent as Shushu's grating voice cut through the chamber's cool air.

"Amun, may your name be praised, the people despair. What must we do to ensure the safety of the Two Kingdoms of Egypt?" the vizier intoned.

There was a pause. Total silence. The distant, familiar sounds of the river. Then a booming voice echoing out from beyond the screen, "Be steadfast. Be courageous. Plant seed prayerfully."

Of course I said nothing out loud, but inside the disrespectful thought welled up – I couldn't prevent it – *"Well, Amun, that's not a lot of help, is it! Can't you do better than that?"* Shocked at my sudden lack of piety, worried that

I might be responsible for disturbing *maat*, I looked around nervously just in case I *had* spoken. Nobody moved. I was safe!

Kamose stepped forward. He's an old man now, a legend in my father's court for his deeds on the field of battle. It's said he has more trophies in his house than any man alive, some of them unspeakably gruesome. Heads, hands, feet and … well, don't ask!

"Will the great god, may his name be ever venerated, hear our prayers and intercede with Hapi to send us rain? For the sake of those who starve. We beseech you, father Amun!"

Another pause. The sound of our hearts beating. What would Amun answer this time? The deep resonant voice came again from behind the veil.

"Rain will come in due season, as I please. The great god Amun wishes only what is good for his people. He will not withhold the flood for ever."

In the semi-darkness, you could touch the disappointment. We needed rain *now*, not sometime later and maybe.

And then Senenmut's voice was heard, measured, smooth and serene, voicing everyone's anxiety:

"Amun, greatest of all gods, we love and adore you. So from where will salvation come for your suffering people? Tell us what we must do, we beseech you!"

At first there was no answer. Then finally the voice from the hidden chamber spoke a third and last time, slow and sonorous. The words he spoke made the hairs on my neck stand up. I shivered. The sound of the god rolled around us like thunder.

"Very well. Then listen, people of Thebes. A running girl will bring prosperity. A young woman will prove the best man in the Two Kingdoms. Honour her. And act on her judgements. If you do this, truly the floods will never fail, and Egypt will fill the earth."

Beside me Nofret gave a gasp. From the corner of my eye I saw her knees give way as she fainted into a little bundle of limbs and linen, out cold on the floor. Instantly Inet was at her side, slapping her face, trying to bring her round. I was rooted to the spot, mouth agape, heart pounding. That phrase. *A running girl.* Who else could Amun have meant but me? No other female I'd ever seen moved at anything quicker than a fast walk. There *were* no other running girls in Thebes, at least not high-born ones. I felt as if every eye had turned towards me and I caught the horrified look on Senenmut's ashen face. *Not* the answer he'd been expecting, I should think. The room swam. My face burned, my legs turned to jelly, and for a moment I thought I'd be joining Nofret on the floor.

Shushu, who would probably rather die than "act on the judgements" of any female, shot a single poisonous look at Senenmut, as if to say "This is all your fault." Then he turned away into his own anger, hunching up the cloak around his shoulders, looking more vulture-like than ever. He rocked backwards and forwards on the balls of his feet, impatient to leave, perhaps afraid the oracle still had more inconvenient things to say. Then, when it was clear the voice had finally fallen silent, he harrumphed loudly and rudely elbowed his way out of the room while the women clucked around Nofret as she stirred and started to vomit. Dazed, and selfishly at that moment more concerned with myself than my sister, I stumbled into the square outside. A great shout went up from all sides to greet the King as he emerged from the temple entrance to bless a wild night of Opet feasting and fun.

But there was to be no celebrating for Nofret and me. Inet swept us up and dragged us back to the harem. "Too much excitement for one day," she exclaimed, as if this was ten years ago, we were still babes in arms and nothing of the least importance had occurred. For once neither of us argued with her. I spent a confused night, tossing and turning, disturbed by dreams where I was running and falling, running and falling, pursued by a cackling, screaming bird intent on pecking out my liver, unable to escape. The bird had a face. It was Shushu's.

The next day, the whole of Thebes was drowsy, full of strong beer and headache after Opet, so it was the day after *that* before I saw Senenmut again. I stood up nervously as he entered the schoolroom. As usual we greeted each other with a bow and folded hands. He looked strained. His eyes were dark and hollowed, as if he'd had no sleep. Morning lessons passed without the subject of the temple prophecy being once mentioned. We didn't talk much at all, and when Senenmut did speak, he was grumpy. Rather than actually teaching me, he just gave me exercises to do, and then grumbled when they weren't perfect, a faulty addition here, a misplaced stroke of the pen there. It was almost as if he was deliberately bringing me back down to earth.

Maybe you're wondering why it's only I who seem to have these lessons in writing and reading, arithmetic and astronomy. "Where's Nofret?" you're asking. "What about the other children in the harem? How come you get Senenmut all to yourself?"

Good questions – and I'm not sure I can give you the complete answers. Senenmut has been my tutor since I was six or seven. Nofret spends all her time with Inet, and has never shown much interest in schoolwork anyway. But then she's been able to weave and cook with a skill I'll never match since she was about five. My brother Wadjmose once had a tutor, it's true, but he's turned seventeen now, and thinks himself the cleverest thing on two legs. He believes he's a real man, even if the fluff on his legs and chin is a regular harem joke. There are other, smaller boys in the harem but although they have lessons, they take them separately. Although my beloved father can seem distant with me, and sometimes speaks roughly on the occasions when I *am* allowed into his presence, I presume the idea came from him. Nofret insists I'm outstandingly clever. Is that right? I haven't a clue – how would you ever know that about yourself?

As Senenmut was about to finish our studies for the day there was a grand arrival outside the entrance to the schoolroom. Shushu's such a noisy person – a mixture of self-importance and clumsiness – that there was no doubt who'd come calling.

"A word, Senenmut," he demanded, from beneath the lintel of the door. No polite morning greeting. Just aggressively to the point. That's the vizier's style.

"Of course," Senenmut replied graciously. "Perhaps outside?" He gestured towards the courtyard.

"Here will do well enough!" Shushu answered. "The girl can hear what I have to say too. I don't want to leave either of you in any doubt."

Up until then I don't think Shushu had ever spoken a word to me directly in my whole life. As far as he'd been concerned I didn't exist. I suppose there'd never been a way I could be useful to him. Over his shoulder I could see Esho's dopey cow-eyes, agog to be the first with a bit of prime gossip. She won't keep the vizier in tow for long, however much she schemes. That tongue of hers is far too loose.

"Let me tell you a story," growled Shushu. The man has

a thin sinister smile constantly playing around his lips. It doesn't mean he likes you. Quite the opposite. "Once upon a time there was a Pharaoh who paid no attention to keeping his harem clean. And so, unknown to him, a nest of horned vipers made their home there. Gradually they took the place over, plotting and scheming, hissing and writhing, determining to strike at the wretched Pharaoh whenever they got the chance. And do you know, Senenmut, they might have succeeded with their plans? They might just have killed the king and replaced him with a snake of their own choosing if it hadn't been for the last-minute intervention of the vizier of the day. Fortunately for that Pharaoh, the vizier discovered the nest in the nick of time, and took a terrible revenge. Afterwards there was nothing and no one left alive. No nest of vipers. Not one, in fact. Not even the smallest baby viper."

He looked at me directly as he spoke the last sentence. I shuddered. I could see the signs of anxiety in Senenmut too, the rubbing of the thumb against the forefinger, a gentle shifting from foot to foot. Shushu was a dangerous and powerful man. No doubt about it.

Senenmut held his nerve. "An interesting story," he replied with apparent calm. "But forgive me for being stupid. Your point is?"

"My point is…" said Shushu icily, his voice a penetrating whisper, "…me, I wouldn't even wait as long as that vizier of old. If there were to be the merest hint of a harem coup, if it were to look for a moment as if a nest of vipers were harboured there, I'd be in with my sharp sword to cut them down in an instant. Like that..."

And he made a single dramatic chop with his right hand to illustrate his words.

For maximum effect, Shushu should have turned on his heel right then and stalked out, but he hesitated, curious to see how Senenmut would react. It was the mark of a weak man, I thought.

"Let me get this right," Senenmut answered, raising his voice so that his words carried out into the echoing space of the harem hall behind Esho. "With all this business about vipers, Shushu, I think you're suggesting that someone in the harem has the power – goodness knows how – to turn the holy oracle of the great god Amun, and persuade him to support a revolution against our lord Pharaoh Thutmose, may he live for ever. Is that correct? And that this "someone" could be me?"

"If the cap fits…"

"You're denying the truth of the oracle? And accusing its priests of treason? Is that what you're saying?"

It was an awe-inspiring moment. Senenmut's voice was thunderous. I wondered if these two great men of the court were about to roll up their sleeves and settle the argument with their fists. Beyond the door, I could see servants pausing in mid-stride to listen. Esho was looking around nervously, aware that a crowd was gathering.

Shushu took a step closer to Senenmut.

"I did not say that…" he said, almost inaudibly. He'd met his match and he knew it.

"I can't hear you…"

"I did not say that…" Shushu snapped.

"I'm sorry? Louder…"

"I did not suggest that!" Shushu's third answer was shouted.

Someone back in the hall sniggered, pleased to see the unpopular vizier in discomfort.

"I'm glad to hear it," said Senenmut, "because people might question your motives, Shushu. But for the record, and so that there *is* no doubt, what was said in the temple came as a complete surprise to me too. And if you were to ask my opinion, I'd suggest that as in all matters to do with oracles, you should take a little time in prayer with the priests to consider the *various* interpretations that could doubtless be made of what was said. Don't you agree? Talk to the experts, that's my advice."

But if Shushu was about to agree, we'll never know, because at that moment an excited Senbi burst into the room. "I'm sorry, my lords," he trumpeted, almost beside himself with glee, "but I bring great news. Great news indeed! Egypt is saved. Holy Amun has heard us. His tears are in great abundance. The Nile-god Hapi has relented. The river is in mighty flood!" And with the swiftest of bows to acknowledge the rank of his hearers, Senbi ran on with a skip and a jump to spread his joyful, life-saving tidings throughout the rest of the harem.

Senenmut raised a theatrical eyebrow at the young guard's enthusiasm. He visibly relaxed and even allowed himself a gentle chuckle.

"Well, Shushu, how about that?" he smiled. "Whatever the oracle's meaning, it seems great Amun isn't too unhappy with the current state of affairs. The *maat* of Egypt must be in good shape after all, regardless of any nonsense about running girls or vipers. Or he wouldn't have released the waters of the Nile to us once more. Would he? Thanks be to Amun for his great mercies, I say!"

Shushu had lost the argument, and he could see it. Contenting himself with a last menacing glance towards me and a muttered, "Yes, yes. Quite so. Thanks be to Amun!" he turned on his heel and flounced out with Esho trotting in his wake, off to check that Senbi's tidings were indeed correct.

I couldn't help noticing that despite his smiling face Senenmut's hands were shaking uncontrollably.

It was about a fortnight later that Mek went missing. Mek's my mongrel dog, a runner like me, a desert animal the colour of sand with the speed of the wind in his long legs. He's affectionate and fun, always begging for scraps of food, a licking, nudging animal. Sometimes, however, a madness gets to him, a faraway look in the eyes, and then we have to watch out.

That afternoon, I saw him suddenly prick up his ears, turn and bolt. He'd probably picked up a call from some girlfriend on the far side of the city that I couldn't hear. When he goes off on these little escapades, I'm always afraid that one day Mek won't come back. After all, there are plenty of people who don't like dogs. On the other hand you hear rumours that some desperate folk occasionally fancy the odd bit of dog for their dinner, although I'd imagine Mek would be a bit stringy for that. More likely someone would just take a shine to him, and, silly mutt that he is, Mek would probably accept a goose-bone bribe and grow old and fat with a new owner who promised him more than I'm prepared to give.

"Where are you going?" Inet's voice faded behind me.

"On a Mek-hunt," I shouted over my shoulder as I picked up speed out of the harem through the gatehouse. "See you later!"

Mek liked putting his nose to the ground in the alleyways of Thebes for the exact reasons I disliked them. There's such a huge range of interesting (to Mek!) and disgusting (to me!) smells down there. On the flat Mek can outrun me any time, and his stamina's far greater too. But in practice, he's always likely to be diverted by various entertainments on the way, scents of other animals, scraps of meat that have been thrown

31

away, an appealing human ankle to sniff. So my chase was a series of tantalizing glimpses of Mek's head and rear bobbing up and down in front of me through the afternoon crowds, always a turn ahead. After fifteen minutes of so of this, I arrived at a T-junction somewhere near the Karnak temple complex. It wasn't a street I knew. I looked left and right past street stalls and chatting women, but Mek was nowhere to be seen. Eeny meeny miny mo. I chose the left-hand direction, and ran on round a bend, only almost to trip over him, leg cocked, peeing up against a house wall.

"There you are, you silly animal," I said tenderly. "Why are you always doing this to me? Shall we go home now, then?" But at the moment when I almost had the collar round his neck, the infuriating Mek ducked sideways and with a furious scrabbling of paws was off again into the narrowest of covered alleys at the end of the little street.

Sometimes the houses of Thebes crowd in so tightly together that their roofs almost close across the tops of the passageways – very good for my sky-skimming. But underneath are many dark, potentially dangerous corners where ideally you'd want an oil lamp to show you the way, and here I had to move forward out of the dazzling sunshine into the smelly, dark alley almost entirely by feel. I waited for a second or two while my eyes accustomed to the gloom and then stumbled forward. I bumped into an end wall, turned right and found myself in the first of what seemed to be a

32

series of rooms with an open corridor down one side. There were enough inscriptions on the walls and decorations on the columns for it suddenly to occur to me that maybe I was in some area at the back of the temple itself. Somewhere close at hand I could hear two men arguing.

Do you believe in coincidence? No, neither do I. I'm sure there's a reason for everything. As I began to make out the sound of the men's voices more clearly I stiffened. One of them I knew immediately by its harsh, sneering tone. Shushu! This time *he* was on the receiving end of a tongue-lashing.

"It's not enough," the other was shouting. His voice was coarse, husky and common, quite the opposite of Shushu's upper-class accent. "Nowhere near enough! It's all very well for you sitting safely in your comfortable office, but this is risky work you're putting me to. And don't forget I've got men to pay – for their silence as well as their labour. So don't you go palming me off with a sack of corn here and a bolt of cloth there. I want a split of the proceeds. Fifty-fifty. It's got to be worth that to you…"

"Listen!" grated Shushu. "I'll say this once and once only. We wouldn't be here having this conversation if you didn't already owe me a favour. With what I know about you, your miserable life could be very rapidly ended. All it takes is a word in the right ear, and you wouldn't exactly be missed. So let's have none of this 'fifty-fifty' nonsense. What we agreed stands. You *will* visit Amenhotep's tomb next week, and you *will* remove *all* the grave goods. My steward will go with you to make an item-by-item inventory which he will then give to me. He will tell you where the goods are to be stored. You'll be paid in corn for one quarter of their value. That will make you a rich man, in the current circumstances. So no funny business. Not if you value your miserable life."

"And the bonuses?" the other man whined.

"*If* everything goes to plan. *If* you aren't caught in the act. *If* I see on the inventory the things I'm expecting."

"And how do I know you'll keep your word?"

"You don't. You have to trust me. If you can't trust a vizier, then who can you trust? Eh?"

There followed more wrangling about payment. I stood there transfixed, suddenly desperate to relieve myself, terrified of being discovered and horrified by what they seemed to be saying. There was only one Amenhotep. And certainly only one whose tomb was worth robbing. That man was my grandfather, now dead for many years and buried in the Valley of the Kings to the west of the River Nile. Could it really be that Shushu was intending to steal from his tomb? How could he think of doing such a wicked thing? To steal a person's grave-goods is to endanger their immortal soul. At very least Shushu was threatening to take away from my grandfather his comforts in the afterlife, and maybe even his very right to live for ever as a god. It made me feel sick that anyone could be so evil.

Meanwhile Shushu was ranting on. "You disgust me,

Paneb!" he was saying contemptuously. "You sordid little people with your jealousies and love of glitter. I'm sure you'd be quite happy melting down any gold you found. Me, all I want is the presence of the old King's cherished possessions close to me in my bedchamber, for their sheer beauty, and so that every night I can absorb a little of his power. But at least I want that power to bring about change and wealth in Egypt for others as well as myself. Whereas you, you're just common criminal vermin, looking out for number one." He drew breath and then snarled. "Meet me here in six days' time, to tell me all is ready. For your sake it had better be!"

I had no idea what treasure could have been buried with Amenhotep – he'd died long before I was born – but Shushu seemed to believe that having the Pharaoh's relics would give him some kind of supernatural authority. Perhaps he was even preparing to claim that the grave-goods had been left to his family by the old Pharaoh as a sign of his right to rule. It occurred to me that the vizier's anxiety about a coup in the harem was just a mirror held up to his own ambition. It was no longer enough to have the ear of the King: Shushu wanted the throne for himself!

In the dusty room, I felt an irritation begin in my nose, and panicking, began to tiptoe away, desperate for the open air, when from the opposite end of the corridor came a familiar friendly greeting, a bark and a whine, and there was Mek charging down over the stone floor to slobber over me as if he'd not seen me for a year. I lost my battle for self-control, and a giant sneeze echoed around the space. It took a second for Shushu and Paneb to realize they'd been overheard, and just a few seconds more for them to pin me by the arms and drag me into the single shaft of light illuminating the floor of the chamber.

"Well, bless my soul!" said Shushu, his mirthless smile curling round the ends of those thin lips. "Talking of bonuses, here's one I really didn't expect. Senenmut's little pupil come to spy on us."

"Ouch," I said, "you're hurting me!"

"Oh, there's plenty worse may happen to you. Do you know what we do to spies, child?"

In spite of myself I answered him with a frightened shake of the head.

"Well, you do surprise me. Senenmut can't be much of a tutor, or you'd know that at least. Clever little girl like you..."

He leaned in to me, so close that I could smell his sour breath, all garlic and bad teeth.

"Let me complete your education. Spies and traitors end up with their throats cut. Isn't that right, Paneb?"

I wriggled, but was held fast. From the corner of my eye I saw Paneb draw an evil-looking knife from under his tunic. Its finely sharpened blade might have been the death of me. Instead it proved to be the conspirators' downfall.

Up until then Mek had been a puzzled observer of events,

sniffing away at one of the walls, thinking perhaps that this was all an elaborate game devised solely for his amusement. But now the glint of the knife somehow registered as a sign of immediate danger in his dog brain. With a sudden gurgling growl he launched himself at a surprised Paneb and sank his teeth into the thug's leg. The knife spun out of Paneb's hand on to the floor. Shushu went to seize it with his left hand, loosening his grip on me as he did so. I kicked him hard in the groin. He yelled with pain and shock, and as his right hand instinctively clutched his stomach, I found myself free. I started to run, first out of the chamber and then in any direction my legs took me, dodging one way and then the other, Mek following in an odd reversal of our earlier chase. I remember crossing an open space into a maze of ancient, dilapidated houses. I was convinced I still heard feet pounding along behind me, but thinking about it now I have no idea whether Shushu and his companion were actually in pursuit – after all, one was temporarily incapacitated by my kick, the other fat and slow. Then suddenly there was the slender figure of a boy my age directly in our path, olive-skinned, curly haired.

"Out of my way," I shouted.

"No, quick. In here!" the boy argued back, and his voice was so compelling I did what he said. His arm guided me to one side, down some steps into a dark, cool space. A finger was put to my lips, and I gathered Mek into myself, my hand over his muzzle to try to keep him quiet while we all crouched down together. From the smell and the straw surrounding us, I guessed we were in a stable.

After a few minutes, when it seemed that any danger of discovery had passed, the boy whispered, "So who was chasing you?"

"Oh … oh … no one! No one in particular…" I blustered. It didn't sound convincing.

"It's all right," he said reassuringly. "You don't have to tell me if you don't want to. You don't look like a bad person. What's it to me if you took a couple of pomegranates or a few vegetables? People have to get by, don't they?"

"I haven't stolen anything," I hissed indignantly. "It was more … personal."

"Running away from home? That's a shame!"

"No!" I said crossly. "Nothing like that at all!"

"Sorry. *Sorry!* My mother always says I ask too many questions. It's a bad habit." The boy fell silent, crestfallen.

"It's OK," I said, mellowing as my pulse rate dropped. Mek pulled away from my hand and licked my face, then licked the boy's too. "He likes you," I laughed. "He doesn't do that with most people."

"Nice dog!" the boy said appreciatively. "What's his name?"

"Mek."

"Mine's Rami – short for Ramses…"

"And I'm Asha."

There was a silence. Neither of us seemed quite sure what to do next. Then Rami said hesitantly, "You look hot. Would you like something to drink? My house is just the other side of that wall."

"Thank you," I said, touched, and suddenly thirsty. "That would be nice."

Although fearful that Shushu and Paneb would suddenly loom from the shadows, I followed him up the steps and round the building to enter through a low doorway. A dark-skinned woman was stirring a pot over a fire in the centre of the room. Her attention was all on her lentil and lamb stew: she didn't look up.

"This is my new friend Asha," said Rami, going to a large jug of beer which stood in one corner of the barely furnished room and straining its golden liquid through a sieve into two drinking bowls. "She's thirsty. Would you like some too, mother?"

"Not for me," the woman answered. Now she stood and smiled at me, massaging her sore back with both hands. "Welcome to our house, Asha! I'm Aneksi, half responsible for bringing Rami into this world. One of the better things I ever did!" And she smiled indulgently at him before returning to her cooking.

There was a low mud-brick bench covered by a woollen rug, two stools, some reed mats, a collection of pots and pans, a little shrine to the household gods Bes and Taweret and not much else. How different from the riches of the harem! These were ordinary people. Poor people, you could say. And yet, this wasn't quite an ordinary house. The walls were covered in paintings. On all sides of us, gods and goddesses danced and played. There was Thoth, and Horus and Seth. There was the River Nile, with boats plying up and down crowded with passengers and goods. And surely, wasn't that a picture of Rami, watching the action from the riverbank? The colours sang. The faces of the people were animated and lifelike. Clasping my drinking bowl in both hands, I wandered around the room admiring, as the real Rami's smiling eyes followed me, enjoying my surprise.

There was a scraping of feet at the entrance. Still frightened by the afternoon's events, I froze and my guts turned to water. But instead of Shushu's mean features I saw the smiling, weather-beaten face of a man some 35 summers old.

"Hello, family. And who's this?"

"Asha," said Rami. "A new friend. Asha, meet my father, Akhpet."

Akhpet studied me carefully.

"You're very welcome, child. But don't I know you from somewhere?"

"I don't think so," I said, too quickly, still spooked by my encounter with Shushu.

"I'm sure I do," Akhpet insisted. "It'll come to me. I'm good with faces. Aren't I, Aneksi?"

"If you say so!" his wife answered teasingly. "You're good at so much, Akhpet. By your own telling..."

She continued to cook, while the rest of us went up to the roof and talked.

"The paintings," I said. "They're wonderful!"

"Thank you," smiled Akhpet. "Really I'm a stonemason, but with each month that passes I seem to be painting more and chiselling less."

"People seek him out," said Rami proudly. "Important people. He makes likenesses so fine, you'd think they were real!"

"Rami exaggerates," said Akhpet, smiling again. "But I *am* good. I won't deny it…"

We talked about pets too, about how they had minds of their own. When Rami was small, the family had lost a favourite dog.

"I was so sad, I cried for days," he said.

And he gazed fondly at Mek, who'd made himself thoroughly at home, lying asleep in the warm sun, legs splayed. There was a long comfortable gap in the conversation. The sounds of the city floated up to us. Everything normal. No commotion. No Shushu. Yet all the time I was aware of Akhpet's intense gaze. It obviously really annoyed him that he couldn't place me. Suddenly he tensed.

41

"Amun have mercy," he exclaimed. "Now I've got it. I suppose I should at least be glad I'm not going senile after all." But the friendly smile had disappeared, and now Akhpet's eyes were anxious, even frightened. "Because of course I *have* remembered where I've seen you before, young woman. You looked very different then – in fact, we admired you as you processed through the streets with your family, didn't we? But tell me, ma'am, how does a daughter of the Pharaoh come to be sitting on the roof of *my* house?"

What a strange afternoon it had been. Without meaning to, I'd come into the possession of information which put me in the greatest danger and on which I had to act, for the sake of my father, as well as myself. And meeting Rami and his family had been unsettling all on its own.

One moment I'd been safe and happy, wrapped up in the warmth of their hospitality: the next it was as if a curtain had suddenly fallen between us. I felt cut off – isolated by an accident of birth. After recognizing me, Akhpet more or less bowed and scraped every time either of us spoke. How could I tell them the truth? Rami's disbelief became obvious as I hesitantly made up a weak story about visiting a sick friend and getting lost. He looked wary, distrustful.

Later I found I couldn't get his sensitive features out of

my mind: the friendly smile, the long dark eyelashes, the cat-like way he moved. It made me unsteady. I'd never felt discontented with who I was before. I wanted more of Rami's company, and knew I couldn't have it. As Mek and I trailed back to the harem, I felt alone and sad, unsure what to do now.

Shushu wasted no time finding me. That same evening, having visited Esho in her room, he cornered Nofret and me. Pretending to bring a personal message from my father, he smarmily requested that Nofret leave us alone for a moment or two.

"Give us the room, will you, my dear?"

She raised an eyebrow, but did as he asked, as slowly and sulkily as she dared. It gave me a moment to gather my thoughts: I had a strategy worked out. If I let him see fear, I reckoned I was a dead girl. The only thing to do was show a bit of attitude.

Shushu came straight to the point. "I can squash you, child, as easily as I squash a wasp," he hissed.

"Wasps sting," I replied, staring him straight in the eye. "Even the smallest ones. Remember who you're talking to, Shushu. I may be young, but I'm the Pharaoh's daughter. I deserve respect. And my father deserves your loyalty."

"What do you know about respect or loyalty? Respect is

earned. So is loyalty. In your little life you haven't yet said or done *anything* to deserve respect. Be warned. Whatever you say against me will be treated with contempt."

"We shall see."

"We certainly shall. If you value your life, you'll be careful not to offend the gods with lies and blasphemy. And very careful not to offend me into the bargain!"

"And *you* should be careful too, Shushu," I said, forcing myself to hold his gaze, concentrating on not blinking. "Fly too close to the sun and it will burn you up!"

Stalemate. I don't think Shushu could believe he'd just been spoken to like that – by a *girl*! His eyes bulged, his nostrils flared, but he was clearly stuck for a suitable reply, and so stalked out. It was only a minor battle, but I'd won!

I knew I had to see my father quickly. Early the next morning I sought a private audience. I said nothing to Senenmut.

"Sit down, child," Thutmose said, not unkindly, but clearly puzzled. "Ahmose tells me you want to see me. Alone. Now, you've never asked for such a thing before, little Asha. Whatever can it be that concerns you so much? Have you fallen in love? Are you pregnant?"

He smiled at his own joke, and I swallowed my annoyance

at his amusement. I was sure my father knew the latter wasn't a remote possibility. Why did even my father assume that these were the only kind of things which might be important to a young princess? Even in fun!

Haltingly, I explained what I'd heard in the temple. His face clouded.

"Asha, these are most serious charges."

"I know. But it's what Shushu said."

"You're sure about that? There was no possibility of mishearing?"

"None at all."

My father drummed his fingers on the table, looked at me, glanced away, studied me again.

"You've never liked him, have you?"

It was a very direct, penetrating question. I was tempted to deny it, to say no, I'd never felt badly about Shushu. But it would have been untrue.

"You're right, Father. I've never liked him."

I paused.

"But then he's never given me reason to. He's always ignored me. And now he threatens me."

"Whereas I've worked with Shushu as my trusted vizier for years. I can't count the number of times I've had reason to be grateful to him."

"I know you believe that."

Thutmose considered for a while and then said decisively,

"Right, there's only one way to sort this out. I must hear what he has to say. In your presence."

Shushu was all smooth charm. The previous evening he'd been a street-fighting scorpion. Now he was a spidery diplomat, spinning his web of deceit – equally lethal.

"A misunderstanding, my lord," he said. "Albeit a most unfortunate one. For some time my officers have indeed been aware of a disgraceful plot to steal from your father Amenhotep's tomb. Yesterday should have seen the coming together of our plans to disrupt the scheme and arrest the criminals. I was on the verge of discovering the names of those responsible, and if your daughter hadn't so regrettably interrupted my interrogation, would doubtless have done so. Sadly that will now be impossible. The birds have flown, and the thief Paneb is certainly beyond reach. At first light he was discovered in a dark corner with his throat cut. Our investigations will need to begin afresh. Be assured, we shall redouble the guard at the tomb itself and spare no efforts to track down the rest of the criminals."

"Hmm," my father said. "I'm glad to hear that, though I'm sorry you didn't see fit to inform me at an earlier stage. And I'm not sure why you felt the need to involve yourself so personally."

"My lord," continued Shushu serenely, "the responsibility of office. There are so many plots, so many evildoers. I try to spare you from all but the most important details."

"I would have thought this a pretty 'important detail'…"

Shushu bowed deeply.

"I stand corrected, sir. It won't happen again. Please accept my deepest apologies. But on another matter, I'm most anxious that the daughter of the Pharaoh shouldn't be put at risk by these little adventures of hers. The area where I discovered her – well, let's just say – is not the *best* neighbourhood. And quite on her own too. One does question the quality of the supervision provided for her. Perhaps some limits to such rash and foolish activity would be sensible?"

In other words, he wanted to keep me in the harem like a good little girl. And my father, bother him, agreed!

"It's no good, child. Shushu's quite right. For your own safety, you must be where we can see you. This running about of yours just won't do, regardless of whether that silly dog of yours goes missing. Send one of the guards to look for the damned animal. It's not ladylike. It's dangerous and it belittles us all. Pharaoh's daughter is no ordinary thirteen-year-old, to be running around the backstreets of Thebes like a street child."

I had to fight the tears. I felt disbelieved and humiliated. By my own father! But there was a sting in the tail for Shushu too. Right there in front of me my father said sternly, before he dismissed us both, "But I want to leave you in no doubt, Shushu, that my daughter's welfare is your final responsibility. Were anything ever to happen to her, you'd be the one to pay. She's very special to me. See she comes to no harm, Shushu! And honour her. Not just because of some prophecy, but for who she is! You understand me?"

Shushu's expression was a picture as he made his final bows and left. Obedience and loathing in equal measures.

Book one
PLANTING

Four months later

When I think about it, if I compare myself with Rami, I'm so very lucky. In lower Egypt, near the northern city of Memphis, great pyramids of stone reach up into the sky and point to the stars. They were built long, long ago to mark the tombs of long-dead Pharaohs. I know this only because Senenmut has described them to me. I've not actually been to visit them. Not yet. Maybe some day soon I will.

But those pyramids are a lesson. Think of the way they're constructed. To be part of the inner circle at Pharaoh's court is to be one of the top stones of the human pyramid. Beneath us, holding us up, is the whole nation of Egypt, millions of human stones, all bearing our weight, helping us to maintain our high position. We have to do nothing for ourselves. If we want food at any time of the day, it's cooked and brought to us – the very best ingredients, spices from the four corners of the world, dill, cumin and coriander; meat every day if we want it, pork, beef and tender lamb, vegetables cleverly prepared, wine of ancient vintages, beer brewed by experts.

Our clothes are all of the finest linen, woven with the deftest of touch, set off by jewellery inlaid with the rarest desert metals and stones. These beautiful clothes are washed and pressed by people we never meet and are brought to us fresh as new each day.

My father's palaces are strewn beside the entire length of the great River Nile. Even though they're fashioned from the same humble mud-brick as a peasant's house, they speak of power and wealth. Each one stretches for hundreds of paces, and is two or three storeys high. Within them the precisely laid floors of the long corridors lead on to patios of pale pink and ochre-hued stone that was once quarried far out in the desert and dragged in on sledges, piece by piece. The patios are shaded by sycamores and fragrant trees of frankincense, whose seeds were originally brought from the distant land of Punt. Weighty stone obelisks commemorate the great deeds of our ancestors and mark our exits and entrances. Hundreds, even thousands of days' work has gone into fashioning each one. Our furniture is the product of teams of carpenters, each chair, stool and bed lovingly carved. Even our tombs are prepared from the time of our birth, chiselled from the bare rock to ensure our safe passage to the next world.

And all we within the palace have to *do* is to be us. All we have to worry about is that we preserve *maat* by making the right decisions and governing wisely. And even then, to help accomplish this task we have the advice of huge armies of civil servants and scribes who know everything that could be possibly known about the world.

Chief of the civil servants is Shushu the vizier, which makes his ambition all the worse. Like me he has everything he ought to want. And yet the desire for absolute power is written all over his mean face. He's *such* a dangerous man. I don't know why my father can't see it. Maybe one day Senenmut will take Shushu's place. Now wouldn't that be a major boost to *maat*!

Meanwhile Rami and his parents, like millions of other stones in the great Egyptian human pyramid, struggle to stay in one piece, sometimes almost crushed by the weight of their tasks. If the Nile-god Hapi withholds the Nile flood, if Amun denies us, if the crops fail, the Akhpets of this world will be the first to suffer from famine. Unlike me they have to work all the hours there are from birth to death, down on their knees, digging, building, washing and cooking till their hands are calloused and torn.

I couldn't help wondering about Rami. I badly wanted to see him to thank him properly for his kindness, but it was hard to see how. Since that first meeting, I'd known we were going to be important for each other. Don't ask me how. I just knew.

For many days and months after the stand-off with Shushu, I was virtually a prisoner in the harem, watched from morning till night by Inet, by my mother Ahmose and even by dear Senenmut. I played along with their game, although I was seething inside, hoping that eventually they'd tire of watching me and I'd be allowed a longer leash. Maybe then, I thought, I'd see Rami again.

So that they knew my spirit hadn't been broken, I trained harder than ever. Each day I spent my spare hours sprinting up and down the length of the harem colonnades, lifting my legs high, repeating the run until I could do twenty repetitions and still not be out of breath. Some days, just to spite them, I took off all my clothes and trained naked. My mother was mystified and put it down to "silliness", while some of the girls professed to be shocked at my "lack of modesty". Nofret told me not to push my luck. Senenmut smiled in amusement and shook his head.

Since I was a baby my aunt Kasmut has been a great friend, and never more so than during those days of imprisonment. Kasmut is married but childless. I think it's probably true that I'm the child she always wished for. Anyway, she's been very kind. She gossiped with me endlessly, chaperoning me on walks down to the river, encouraging me to stay strong.

"Men may think they rule the world," was her constant refrain, "but we women know they can't survive a day without us. All those big chaps are just little boys at heart. Inside they're crying for their mothers because they can't immediately, this minute, have the exact thing they want. Our job is to pat them on the head, tell them it's all right, croon them to sleep, and gently lead them into more reasonable ways. It's true, Asha. Women are the stronger sex, you know!"

Senenmut would sometimes walk out with me too, showing me the building that was going on while the Nile was in flood, helping me understand the engineering of the irrigation projects which gradually, year by year, stretch the fields in an ever wider arc on both sides of the river by the city.

One day we'd been down at the riverside to see how the waters were beginning to slacken after three full months in spate, leaving ever more obvious margins of fertile black silt. A few farmers were paddling on the muddy new beach, leaning on their sticks, stroking their chins and discussing the right time to move in and plant the season's first crops.

We'd finished watching and were strolling back to the harem on the approaches to the dark alleyways at the edge of the city. As we ducked into the street out of the harsh light we were temporarily blinded, and in that moment there was a sudden rush from our left. I heard Senenmut's grunt as he doubled up, caught off guard by a blow to the stomach.

There were two assailants and they'd misjudged their target. With his domed forehead and slight stoop, Senenmut might look like a scholar, and perhaps older than he really is, but I've seen him wrestle, and actually his body isn't any weaker than his mind. He's every bit the equal of some of the younger harem guards, and they're supposed to be trained killers.

So even though he was surprised and winded by the attack he still had the presence of mind to call out to me, "Run, Asha!"

I'm not sure I believe in heroes. What I think happens at moments like that is that something in the brain takes over. There's no time to ask yourself, "*Shall I be brave then?*" You just act. So although it was probably a stupid thing to do, I ignored Senenmut.

In the next seconds, as one of the two men aimed a kick at his head, Senenmut seized the incoming ankle and twisted it viciously upwards to take his attacker off balance and throw him to the floor. I glimpsed a threatening sliver of metal in the hand of the other thug, and shouted, "A knife, Senny. To your right…", but Senenmut was there well before my warning, slamming the hand against the wall so its weapon clattered to the ground, simultaneously raking his left forearm across the attacker's face, the point of the elbow piercing an eye, the fist splintering a cheekbone as it came one way, driving deep into the jaw on its return. The man dropped like a felled date palm. The first attacker had now understood what he was up against, and was making a desperate escape, half crawling, half running up the alley on a damaged hamstring.

Senenmut put his hands to his knees, breathing heavily, blood from his nose smeared across one cheek.

"Are you all right, Asha?"

"I'm fine. What about you?"

"I'll live."

"Who were they?"

"Good question. They were waiting for us, whoever they were."

"And why would they think we were carrying anything worth stealing?"

"Exactly. Since they must have been watching us, they'd have known we *weren't*, wouldn't they?"

"A mystery…"

"Food for thought. But probably not much of a mystery."

"Shushu?"

"You're too wise for your years, Asha. But at the moment just think it. Don't say it. You may be right, but we'll have to bide our time…"

During the afternoon I didn't feel at all affected by the shock of what had happened, but by early evening I was dull and tearful. A painful, throbbing headache had set in, and I went to bed early, for all the good it did me. I spent the first part of the night in a maddening tumble of dreams. I was on a boat sailing up the Nile. Senenmut was there and so were my family. My father was in the prow, staring upstream, ignoring everyone else, his eyes fixed on the horizon. And although the waters were calm, and the boat was perfectly stable, I kept slipping off its edge into the sludgy water, drawn by some powerful unseen force in its depths. I stretched out for Senenmut's hand, but he couldn't hold me. My arms and legs were pinned to my sides. I felt myself falling and drowning, turning over and over, my plait of hair waving above me as I struggled for breath. And then, out of nowhere, there was Rami, smiling and suntanned, beckoning to me, pulling me to safety on the bank. But when I reached out to touch him, he'd gone, and I was left alone on a muddy beach, my feet sinking into the silt, unable to touch bottom.

I woke suddenly and sat upright. Frustrated, I thumped the brick wall with my fist, annoyed that when I wanted it most, I couldn't get to sleep. Little flakes of plaster fell off, and guiltily I tried to stick them back on again. My mind cleared, and I found I was angry that even after the oracle's dramatic words, I'd been put away out of sight under house arrest. Hadn't the god said I was to be "honoured"? And hadn't my father repeated that instruction to Shushu? Well, this was no way to "honour" anyone, was it?

I believe in the hidden truth of dreams, don't you? In my nightmare Rami had come to me. So maybe, I began to think, I should answer his beckoning call. Maybe it was a sign that he'd keep me safe in the middle of all this trouble. After all, he'd rescued me once before, hadn't he? Mad as it seemed, I'd go and seek out Rami as soon as I could, whatever anyone said, in the hope that he'd be there for me when I needed him, and help me fight back against Shushu and my father.

As soon as I could at first light, slightly self-consciously, I went and found Senbi.

"When are you next on the early morning guard shift?" I said, trying to sound casual.

He immediately looked at me suspiciously.

"What do you want?" he said bluntly.

"A blind eye," I answered. "Puh-lease, Senbi? Just for a couple of hours. No one will know I'm gone, I promise."

"You want me to end up on a charge?" he said. "It really is more than my life's worth, you know."

"I won't let you down," I said, and let my lip tremble slightly. "There's something I must do outside the palace, or I'm going to go crazy."

"Oh all right," he said, relenting. "Tomorrow. But if you

can, make sure I *really* don't see you go, so that I don't have to lie to anyone! I'll leave the East Gate door unlocked."

"You're a good friend to me…"

"I'm a fool to myself…"

I slipped out of the East Gate door before the sun was up, and half ran, half walked in the direction I thought would lead me to Rami's house, arriving there as the sun rose. At one point on the journey everything seemed suddenly unfamiliar, and I was convinced I'd taken a wrong turn, but then I saw a butcher's shop I recognized, and shortly afterwards the stable where Rami and I had taken shelter. There was a clatter of pots from the kitchen as I knocked softly at their door. Aneksi opened it, and when she saw me, dropped to her knees in a curtsey.

"You don't need to do that," I said. "How are you, Aneksi? And Akhpet? Is he well?"

"We're fine, thank you, ma'am," she answered cautiously, her dark eyes curious to know what I was doing there, and so early in the day too. "*You're trouble, you are!*" they seemed to say.

"Look, Aneksi," I said apologetically, "I know it's very early – but I'm looking for Rami. Is he here?"

Aneksi bowed and replied, "I'm afraid not, ma'am. He's working with his father over in the Valley of the Kings. They'll be away a month or so. Akhpet says there's an important job to do. But I'm expecting them back after that to help with the harvest. It's National Service, you know, ma'am."

I tried to hide my deep disappointment, although in my heart I knew my dream had suggested Rami wouldn't be so easily found. If I really wanted to see him, some obstacle or other would have to be overcome. Just how important was it to me?

All the men take turns on helping with projects for the state. They're called at least once a year, most of them to be simple labour on building works, although if they have special skills, particularly in something like stonemasonry or painting, they may go more often. I knew there was a permanent workmen's village in the Valley of the Kings. That must be where Rami and Akhpet were.

"Well," I said sadly, "if Rami comes back in the next week or so to visit, will you tell him that Asha was asking after him?"

"I will, ma'am. If you wish it."

"I'd like that very much."

And that was where the conversation ended. I could see she wasn't happy with me in her house, and I didn't know what else to say, so I waved goodbye and dragged myself away.

But even while I was walking back to the harem, a plan began to form. If it was to work, I'd need my aunt Kasmut's help. At the East Gate Senbi looked relieved to see me returning safely.

"If you wanted, there is one other thing you could do for me," I said. "Nothing complicated, just a message taken."

"Must I?" he said.

"I'll put a good word in for you with Nofret…"

Senbi blushed.

The message reached Kasmut and later she came to see me. She looked me up and down with a critical eye, and said, "You don't seem quite yourself? Are you OK, Asha?"

"Well," I replied, "there could be several reasons for that."

And I explained about the assault on Senenmut, about our suspicions of Shushu's involvement and my previous encounter with Rami. Then I told her my plan, and how she could help.

"No," she said firmly. "This is silly, Asha. You're my favourite niece and I love you to pieces, but honestly, you really can't be serious about running the length and breadth of Egypt dressed as a boy, looking for this young man. Firstly it won't fool anyone for a moment, secondly it's undignified, and thirdly it's completely unnecessary. What's so special about the lad anyway? Are you thinking of marrying him?"

"Goodness, no!"

"Well don't look at me like that! It's not a *completely* stupid question. Since you *are* just about a woman now, you could very shortly get married, and you wouldn't be the first obstinate Pharaoh's daughter to insist on wedding a commoner. But even though you're clearly not at *all* in love with this Rami, tell me about him. Is he very handsome?"

I reddened and told what I knew.

"...I'm just sure he and his family are going to be important to me. Don't ask me how I know. I just do. OK? Oh look, if you really want to know, I had a dream."

"Fine! Well, that makes it all *so* much more sensible then. Look, Asha, if we're to trust these dreams and intuitions of yours, there are better ways of dealing with the matter. When your father next eats with us in the harem, we'll ask permission to take you to the west bank of the river to visit your grandad Amenhotep's temple. For old times' sake, Thutmose won't refuse me. And Shushu won't be around to protest. While we're over there we'll make some discreet enquiries about Rami and his father, and see if we can't find you two some time together. How does that sound?"

I told her she was the best aunt ever.

"Aren't I just? And now, listen to some advice from 'the best aunt ever'. First lesson. Being a woman is good. We live longer than men. Thank Amun, we think with our hearts and not with our fists. We have wisdom as well as wit. Second lesson. Being the principal daughter of the Pharaoh is much, much better than simply good. You know you'll always be precious to him, and you're guaranteed his love and protection. He'll never see *you* as a threat, as he might some upstart young son."

"My father doesn't think of Wadjmose or Edjmet as 'threats', does he?" The thought had never crossed my mind before. I was shocked.

"Who knows? Sometimes I think the blood that flows through men's veins is quite different from ours…"

When the King comes to the harem, every ten days or so, there's a feast. It's a day I like. Under my mother Ahmose's instructions, we spend the day preparing, helping with the food, laying the tables, deciding who'll sing or dance for him and teaching each other new songs. It brings people together. When I dance everyone laughs. They tease me and say I'm all arms and legs, that I remind them of a jumping spider. Inet takes it personally. "I've tried, Amun knows I have," she moans, "but despite all my efforts that girl has never learnt the meaning of 'graceful'." However, Inet can't complain about my singing, because actually I'm rather good. I hold a melody well, and if someone gives me the words, I find a new tune will often just float into my head. The ruder and funnier the words, the better my brain seems to work. Soppy lyrics make my mind go blank. Unlike Kasmut, Inet doesn't share my sense of humour.

On this occasion the Pharaoh was in a very good mood. He'd just received a report that our armies had defeated the King of Mitanni in a mighty battle near the River Euphrates far to the north-east.

"We got 'em," he chortled. "Heaps of enemy corpses everywhere. That'll teach them to raid our hunting grounds. Talking of which," he said, waving a hand in the vague direction of my mother, "I'm taking your son off for a spot of hunting. We may be away a month or so. Young Wadjmose has been looking a bit pasty-faced – he could do with some fresh air. Let's see if we can catch us a lion or two. Besides, there's some business to be done up north. They're building us a new palace up at Memphis, and a visit from the Pharaoh will help buck up their ideas."

My mother looked doubtful. The words "Do be careful, darling!" were probably on her lips, but of course it wasn't her place to say them. Wadjmose puffed out his chest. If he felt anxious at the thought of stalking a lion, he wasn't going to show it.

Perhaps it was fortunate that the song I'd chosen to sing (at Kasmut's suggestion) was about the bravery of men on horseback, the loving bonds between animal and rider:

You carry me, beloved animal,
At the speed of the mountain wind
Across raging torrents of water,
Through the burning desert,
Even as night falls,
Uncomplaining,
And more loyal than any human friend.

It all sounded a bit much to me, but Kasmut had been sure the plaintive melody would soften my father up, and she was right. As I let the last notes hang in the air, I saw my father surreptitiously wipe a tear from his eye, and he called out across the room, "Beautiful, my little skylark, beautiful…"

Kasmut clutched my arm and whispered, "No problem now. You'll see. You've got him eating out of your hand. Maybe you should ask him for a gold bracelet as well while you're at it!"

But I decided not to push my luck, and left satisfied with his permission for our overnight visit to the west bank. Purely to pay our respects to my grandfather, of course.

"And be sure to make a diversion into the Valley to see how they're getting on with my tomb, while you're about it, little bird. I'll expect a full report when I get back!" my father yelled. Our best Mediterranean wine had done its work.

Dad had just given us the perfect excuse for going wherever we wanted.

Ahmose tutted. She didn't share my father's enthusiasm for tomb-building. Not when the tomb in question was his own.

Choosing a lucky day, six or seven later, Kasmut and I set out from the harem across the city to board the northern Nile ferry. With us came Senbi and a maid to carry our bags and look after us. Word had been sent ahead to the custodians at Amenhotep's temple that accommodation should be prepared for us. Senbi had collected the necessary passes for entry to the Valley of the Kings from Shushu's office the previous day.

"He's not a happy chap," Senbi remarked. "You should have seen his face. What's it to him if your aunt Kasmut wants to take you up there?"

I didn't enlighten him.

Once the ferry has glided into the little harbour on the Nile's west bank, it's a short walk to Amenhotep's temple, set back from the river not far from the workmen's village, under the shelter of the high river cliffs. While a priest proudly showed us around the temple's beautifully decorated outer courts, Senbi traipsed up into the village to see if he could discover

Akhpet and Rami's whereabouts. The maid was led off to inspect our tents.

"Your grandfather was such a wonderful man," Kasmut whispered, as we strolled around, trying to admire the temple courtyards. "I still miss him, you know. You'd have loved him too. He had a fantastic, rude sense of humour. A bit like yours, actually. This place is so polite and tidy that it doesn't feel like him at all. Maybe it would be different if we were allowed to go further inside…"

The priest overheard her. His brow furrowed. He suddenly looked concerned.

"Oh, don't worry!" Kasmut laughed. "I know the rules. I'm not suddenly going to run into the holy of holies and lose you your job. But it *is* frustrating. I wonder if we'd catch more of a sense of your grandfather near his tomb?"

"The tomb itself is quite close by, ma'am," said the priest. "Particularly if you take the path from the village. It's at this end of the Valley."

Kasmut nodded her thanks.

Back outside, we encountered Senbi.

"What's the news?" I asked.

"Well, it seems as if Akhpet and Rami are probably at the camp over in the Valley, not at the village. Their work is at such a level of importance that apparently they're very rarely seen there."

I raised an eyebrow at Kasmut. "Lots of reasons for a visit to the Valley then!"

The next morning we rose early. You could walk to Amenhotep's tomb easily in a single hour, and on to the workmen's camp in another, although it wouldn't be very comfortable in the heat of the day because the path up from the village is so steep, winding and rocky. Security was intense, and there were guards and checkpoints everywhere. Everyone who comes and goes from the Valley is searched, and their names are written down. It's a strange twilight world, because no one can be trusted. "*Even those guards inspecting our passes might be in Shushu's pocket,*" I thought to myself.

The Valley of the Kings is a very special and sacred place, but it attracts evil. It's somewhere you speak quietly for fear of disturbing the peace of the dead, yet where murder and robbery are not unknown. Even the exact location of the tombs is a mystery unless you're one of the chosen few. The entrances themselves have been well hidden. Who knows, there might be one behind that rock, or under that flat area of ground. And within the tombs, rumour has it there are many false doors and passages with dead ends to confuse would-be robbers.

"Doesn't this place give you the creeps, Kasmut?" I asked, shivering despite the rapidly increasing heat of the day.

"Doesn't it worry you to be so outnumbered by the dead? I don't want to turn a corner and bump into a ghost."

"Well, if it's your grandad, at least you know it'll be a friendly ghost!"

"And what about Shushu?" I said, suddenly unnerved. "What if he decides to come and get us? There's no shortage of places to dispose of a few bodies up here!"

"Listen to me," said Kasmut sternly. "Are you a princess of Egypt or not? You're quite safe, Asha! Senbi won't let any harm come to us. And anyway, if anything bad were to happen to you now, the first place your father would send the palace guard would be Shushu's office, and he knows it. But if you're still worried, pray to your grandfather for his protection."

In my head I did as I was told, and the prayer must have worked, because my panic immediately began to subside, and I started to remember what I was there for. As I cheered up, I realized it was really good to be out of the harem and out in the clear desert air. For the first time in weeks I felt free.

"I'm going to stay here for a while," said Kasmut when we'd reached the approximate site of Amenhotep's tomb, in a shady ravine which led off the main Valley. "I'm quite happy to be by myself with my thoughts. Why don't you and Senbi go and find Rami?"

In the worker's camp a foreman was surprised to see a princess arriving on his patch.

"I know who you mean, ma'am," he said. "As it happens, Akhpet and his son are working on your father's tomb. I'll take you there." There was a pause, and the hint of a twinkle. "Rami's a fine young man," he said. I blushed.

He led us along a track, maybe another thousand paces. Then the path turned steeply up the hillside again, and suddenly we were scrambling across boulders and rubble on our hands and knees. As we hauled ourselves over a little ridge I saw a gang of men with hammers and chisels in their belts, pulling lumps of stone this way and that on a levelled plot of ground.

The foreman greeted them and asked for Akhpet. One of them pointed at a shaft which sloped away sharply into the ground on the far side of the small plateau. The men stared at me, and I stared back.

"*This is no place for a slip of a girl,*" their faces said. Perhaps they thought my presence would bring them bad luck.

"Mind your head, ma'am," said the foreman, as we stooped to enter the shaft. Oil lamps dimly lit the way down, and where the passageway turned, the temperature dropped suddenly. I drew my shawl more tightly around my shoulders. There were several more twists and turns before the passageway opened out into a chamber. Kneeling on the floor was Akhpet, concentrating fiercely on the delicate black outlines of a procession of figures painted on to the wall. Beside him squatted Rami, holding a pot of paint in one hand and a selection of reed brushes in the other. I could make out the horns of the goddess Hathor at the procession's head. Lovely Hathor. My favourite immortal.

"She's beautiful," I said softly. "Hello!"

Our greeting was awkward. The foreman and Senbi hovered, not knowing whether to go or stay. Akhpet stood, half bowed, stumbled and clutched his back. It suddenly came to me that the work of even a master artist was uncomfortable, and distinctly unglamorous. The cold, the lack of light, the aching muscles! Rami looked shy.

"It's all right," I smiled at the foreman. "You can leave us now! Senbi, do you mind waiting for me at the entrance?"

"It's a surprise to see you, ma'am," said Akhpet.

"And I didn't expect to find you here, either," I answered, which was partly true. I hadn't. Not in my father's tomb. I explained that my father had asked me to give him a progress report.

"Well," said Akhpet, not looking any more comfortable for that piece of news, "why don't you show the Princess around, Rami? I can manage on my own for a while."

There were four or five chambers, some as yet undecorated, one or two seemingly fully prepared. Beautiful friezes ran around the walls: recollections of bloody battles, with the soldiers of Egypt's enemies, Nubians, Assyrians, Mitanni, all in frantic retreat from our swords and spears; pictures of prosperity in the city and the countryside, crops being harvested, flour ground, cattle tended, vineyards planted; people celebrating, stuffing themselves with food, dancing for joy and making music. And in every scene, a figure far larger and more grand than anyone else presiding over the action – the beaming face of my father applauding Egypt's overwhelming success.

"They're fantastic," I said. "How much of it is your dad's work?"

"A lot of the planning," Rami answered proudly, "particularly in this room and the one you saw before. The palace artists' department tells him what's needed, and he makes the sketches on the walls. Then, can you see how the masons have carved back the stone to make the pictures stand out in relief? Well, when they've done that, the painters move in, and maybe a year later, my father comes back to finish the outlines, as we're doing now."

"I never realized it took so long," I said. "But if your father only does some of the work, who does the rest, and how does it fit together so well?"

"There are many master painters," Rami answered. "It's a craft handed down through the generations. Fathers talk to sons, as Akhpet has talked to me. We know how things should look because we always have the best of the old masters to refer to. Only the artists themselves can really tell who did what."

Looking at a scene of a small gathering of people sitting

on couches around the Pharaoh, the figures draped in gorgeous reds, yellows and blues against a grey background, I gasped in amazement. "Isn't that my mother?" I said. "And me? And Wadjmose? You've made us look so perfect. I'm nothing like as pretty as that!"

"You must have had your likeness painted many times?"

"Yes. But not always so flatteringly!"

"But not always by Akhpet! He only has to see a face once, remember. He can lock it in his memory, then take it out and redraw it months later. He's training me to do the same. It's hard, but I'm getting better. And in your case, he's not just relying on someone else's sketch. He's actually met you!"

"What about the rooms that haven't been painted yet? Who are they for? When will work begin on them?"

Rami looked reluctant, his eyes shyly downcast.

"They're for … lesser members of the royal family," he said, choosing his words carefully.

His meaning slowly sank in.

"The *lesser* members? You mean … for someone like me…? *My* tomb?"

He didn't answer. Suddenly the room felt a little colder still.

Akhpet, perhaps embarrassed to be entertaining a royal guest underground, said it was time for breakfast, and we made our way back to the surface. Outside now, the sun was higher in the sky, and the day was getting hotter by the minute. Akhpet shared milk, bread and cheese with the other craftsmen under the shade of an awning while Rami and I walked out on to a wide rock ledge where we could see the whole valley displayed before us.

"I didn't *just* come to see my father's tomb," I said as we watched the figures dotted around the valley floor, the laden donkeys toiling up the tracks, the small collections of brightly painted buildings glistening in the sharp morning light. "I wanted to see you again."

Rami said nothing.

"I know it sounds silly," I continued. "But I think … meeting you … it was for some bigger reason…"

Two falcons, royal birds, were riding the wind high above us. Rami shaded his eyes to watch them as they circled higher and higher, catching the thermals.

"It's not at all silly," he answered eventually. "I've always thought so too."

I caught his hand and held it. He jumped as if he'd been stung by a bee, but didn't let go. I felt warmth and energy pass between us, and in those few seconds, my *ka* regained strength and purpose. Everything would be all right.

"Well that's good then," I said. "Now we just have to find out why, don't we? Remember – whatever happens, don't be a stranger, Rami!"

As the ferryboat began its slanting journey across the current back to the Nile's east bank Kasmut asked, "Mission accomplished?"

"A beginning," I said.

"Of what?"

"Don't ask me!"

"But time well spent?"

"Definitely. So thank you, Kasmut. I feel much better. The fresh air has helped too!"

We exchanged smiles. I leaned back against the side of the boat and trailed a hand in the waters of the river. The knots in my stomach were unravelling. For those few minutes under the warmth of the afternoon sun it seemed as if life was coming right. My personal *maat* was in good shape. But that state of affairs wasn't to last even as far as nightfall.

Book one
HARVEST

We hadn't even set foot inside the harem that dreadful day when a distraught Nofret fell upon us, throwing herself from side to side, clutching her head, crying a river of tears.

"What on earth's the matter?" Kasmut asked her. "Come on, child, tell us!"

"It's Wadjmose," she sobbed. "I'm so sorry, Asha. He's dead."

Inside the palace there was uproar. The news of Wadjmose's death had been brought to Thebes by a messenger: my father was still on his miserable way home from the north. My mother was distraught. What I've not told you is that she and Thutmose had already lost one much-loved son. My older brother Anenmose passed away from a fever when I was six and he was sixteen. Now Mother was wailing that she must be cursed. She couldn't think what she'd done to deserve being deprived of two such fine upstanding boys. I remembered the times I'd nursed bad thoughts about Wadjmose when he'd been horrible to me, and begged every god I could think of for forgiveness.

"Is it all my fault?" I cried as I clung to Kasmut for support. "Did I bring this about somehow?"

"No, Asha," she replied. "That's just superstition and guilt. Awful things happen in this life, but whoever or whatever's to blame, it's not you. Dry your tears. For your father's sake, you've got to be as brave as you can."

I questioned Senenmut to see what he knew of the circumstances.

"A freakish hunting accident," he said. "Inexplicable. Unbelievable. You wouldn't think it possible an arrow could go astray like that – to kill a royal prince?" He shook his head. "Why weren't they paying better attention?"

"Whose arrow?" I said, startled, seeing the possibility of even worse news to come. "Tell me it wasn't my father's?"

"No, no. Thank Amun for that at least. I'm told one of the courtiers was responsible. There was the sudden sighting of a lion, he drew his bow unwisely … and that was it."

"And it *was* an accident?"

There was the merest flicker of hesitation and then Senenmut answered, "No reason to think otherwise, Asha. But we must wait and see."

Two days later word came that my father was shortly to arrive, and we all stood to greet him as his silent procession entered the palace gates. I was shocked at the way he looked.

In two weeks he'd aged ten years. His face was grey and lined, his shoulders were hunched, and as he dismounted his limbs were stiff and clumsy. As he stumbled into the palace, the official mourners who flanked him began their keening, wailing chant – the music of another world.

For a month the palace became a sombre, quiet place. People spoke in hushed tones. Simple white linen clothes were laid out for us to wear. We ate the plainest food. The embalmers had already started work on Wadjmose's body close to where he'd fallen. Soon he would be brought slowly south so that the process could be completed in Thebes. In 70 days' time we would watch him begin his last earthly journey across the Nile to his final resting place, perhaps to be sealed in one of the rooms I'd just seen on my visit to Rami. I thought of those words: *for the lesser members of the royal family*, and shuddered again. When he'd spoken I'd wondered if it had been a sort of prophecy. But I'd misunderstood. The words hadn't been for me – not this time.

If Wadjmose's death had been a shock, an even greater one was on the way. At our first class in a while, Senenmut said rather too casually that my father had asked to see me. On my own. A warning trumpet sounded in my head. My stomach fluttered. This had never happened before.

"Why?" I asked Senenmut suspiciously.

"I don't know, madam."

"And Senenmut, why are you calling me madam? Asha's always done perfectly well before! It'll do in the future!"

Senenmut bowed meekly, and I realized I'd spoken more sharply than I should have done to my friend and tutor.

"I'm sorry, Senny. I didn't mean to be rude. You know the way it's been recently … but I don't understand…"

He looked at me gravely, and spoke softly.

"Asha, perhaps things are going to be different from now on. I hope Your Highness and I will always share a good relationship … but in public … sometimes a little formality…"

"Your *Highness*? Senenmut, you're worrying me. Please explain yourself."

"Just consider, Asha. With your brother Wadjmose so tragically killed, mightn't Edjmet be the proper successor to your father's throne?"

Senenmut's words fell like stones on my head. Edjmet? My half-brother? Lopsided, spotty, weak-in-the-head Edjmet, endowed with the physical grace of a pig and the conversational skills of a baboon? Edjmet to be Pharaoh one day? Was there no one else?

"There are other princes…"

"They may all be thought to have weaknesses which would disqualify them, Asha.

"And I suppose Edjmet has no weaknesses?"

Senenmut spread his hands, not arguing the point. But there was worse to come.

"When you talk with your father, you should perhaps be prepared for the possibility, Asha, that as your parents' only surviving child, with your fourteenth birthday shortly to be celebrated, your marriage to Edjmet might now be thought a most suitable thing. Egypt's *maat* might be best preserved by such a union. Wouldn't you say?"

I could see his point, *and* was at the same time horrified by the whole idea. And of course realized then, as never before, just how much I cared for Rami.

When I emerged, dazed, from the audience with my father the next day and described to Senenmut what had happened, he smiled wryly.

"Lettuce and stick," he said. "It's what all good rulers do."

"I don't follow you…"

"If you need to get a donkey to work for you…"

"So I'm a donkey now?"

"Well, it works perfectly well with humans too … you're nice to him by feeding him the lettuce, and then you wallop his rear end with a stick."

If I thought about it, I could see what he meant.

When I'd been shown into my father's presence, he'd just

finished consulting with Shushu, who left us promptly with a deep bow to the King and a sarcastic nod of the head to me.

My father's eyes followed Shushu as he backed out of the room. He waited until the vizier was out of earshot and then began to speak.

"Don't worry about *him*," he said. "Shushu has his plans and I have mine. The difference is that there's only one Pharaoh. And he's not it. Sit down, daughter."

I pricked up my ears. This was a change too. Up to now I'd always been "child" or "little Asha". To be called plain "daughter" was new. And somehow more official.

"I've been thinking," he said wearily, though it was as if the thought was completely unconnected to Wadjmose's death, "it's time you continued your education in here with us. I've decided I'd like you to sit with me in court every few days from now on. Senenmut will accompany you. He's such a wise counsellor for you, and I hope that will always be so. I know you two see eye to eye. But you need to understand how decisions are made and how to administer justice, and you can't get that from Senenmut's lessons. Some day, you may need to know how to rule."

And then he added, as if it was an afterthought, "And perhaps we should have Edjmet along too. He's a dear boy, if a little slow. Perhaps I haven't given him the opportunities I should have. Wadjmose … you know … had all my hopes…"

80

My father swallowed hard, paused, and looked away a moment to compose himself. He unclenched his jaw and turned back to me. His eyes were damp.

"I haven't forgotten the Opet oracle, daughter. In fact, these last weeks, I've thought much about it … the loss of Wadjmose, your growing into womanhood. Asking myself if it was a coincidence, or if father Amun was telling me something…"

I felt I had to speak, to offer him some comfort.

"Who can truly interpret the ways of the gods, father? We have to be faithful. Make our offerings. And try our best to understand."

He studied me thoughtfully and smiled wanly.

"A devout answer, daughter. A politician's answer too. You'll do well."

He sat up a little straighter.

"Now, let's talk of happier things. Tell me, how's your running?"

The change of subject caught me off guard.

"Less frequent and less ambitious, sir," I replied hesitantly, wondering what would please him.

He suddenly roared with laughter.

"I'm very glad to hear it," he said. "But here's an idea that amuses me. Why don't we encourage more of the women to take exercise? I was only thinking to myself the other day that some of the harem were growing very slack and lazy. Take that girl Esho, for instance. Very pretty. But going to seed. She and all the rest should accompany you in your daily routine. Do 'em good. There's a little task for Pharaoh's daughter. Find a way to make it happen."

"Esho seems to find much favour elsewhere, sir," I said cheekily, my heart sinking that my father Thutmose had just found a way to make me so instantly unpopular.

"Now listen," he said, pretending severity, "if you're to hold court with me, you'll have to learn honesty as well as tact. Practise your *diplomacy* on other people – like Shushu – and give *me* your honesty. Esho is growing fat, and we both know it."

"If you say so, father."

Some bunch of lettuce. Some stick!

"It's very clever, though," Senenmut mused. "Think of it. On the one side, you, the Pharaoh's daughter, with me standing behind you. And on the other Edjmet with Shushu to advise *him*. You see how your father so wisely seeks balance."

"*Or is writing a recipe for disaster?*" I thought to myself. Just supposing I could cope with Edjmet's spots and appalling manners, would the two counsellors ever be able to play nicely?

So for the next 40 days or more, every day or so, I began to sit with my father and Edjmet, hearing the petitions of the people passing before him. If I learned one thing, it was that my father had much greater patience than I did. He'd listen intently while foreign ambassadors or petty officials from Memphis droned on about which piece of useless desert land belonged to whom, or what the latest forecasts for grain production were. Mentally I often found myself saying, *"Yes, yes, now just get to the point, will you?"* while Thutmose seemed to manage to stay genuinely interested. At least I was doing better than Edjmet. He could barely stifle his yawns. So much did he fidget that I was sometimes seriously worried he'd topple off his chair. And if asked whether he had any questions, Edjmet's answer was invariably a dull, stupid shake of the head, or a vacant, "No, not really."

A pattern seemed to develop in which Edjmet and I were left alone to talk together when these sessions ended. I'd wait for Edjmet to start the conversation, and then, realizing I'd probably die before he'd finished studying his dirty fingernails and picking his nose, would eventually give up and brightly say something like, "Those ambassadors from Punt dress very oddly."

"Don't they just," he'd reply.

"And don't you just hate the stink of that oil they wear?"

"Yes."

"Wouldn't it be fun to visit their country some time?"

"Perhaps."

"What do you think it's like?"

"Don't know…"

"So what did *you* do this morning, Edjmet?"

"Not much, really…"

Was this the future ruler of Egypt? If so, great Amun help us.

"Maybe he's just shy," said Nofret. "You can be quite frightening, Asha … give him some space. I'm sure he'll relax eventually."

But there were no signs of it. Boring, boring, boring. And slightly smelly too.

As time passed, one thing became clear, particularly after the sad day when Wadjmose was finally buried – my father was ailing. Some days he slumped rather than sat on his throne. His gaze was still keen, but the rest of him was shrinking away before our eyes. He rarely seemed to eat or drink. Food and wine had always been a great pleasure for him but now not even my mother's encouraging words and tasty morsels aroused any interest. She'd personally bring him his favourite foods, marshmallows, toasted nuts, the finest dates dipped in brandy, but he'd make only a token effort before pushing the bowl aside.

The last rites for Wadjmose were private and dignified. Perhaps it would have been better if there'd been a traditional state funeral with pomp and ceremony. Perhaps it would have released the grief that was poisoning my father from inside. Wishful thinking had taken him over. His grip on reality was slipping away.

"You two seem to be getting on so well," he declared one day about me and Edjmet. (There was absolutely no evidence for this.) "Do I feel romance in the air?"

And then a few days later, still kidding himself…

"What little lovebirds! You two are so obviously made for each other. I can't tell you how happy this makes me. We must begin to make the marriage arrangements. No point in delay, is there? We must be happy now, mustn't we? Eh, Edjmet? Eh, Asha? What do you think, Shushu?"

Edjmet gave his idiot giggle. At least he was pleased.

"It *is* the right thing to do," Senenmut insisted in private to me, "although I know it's not what you *want* to do. This nation may shortly need you as its Queen."

"Senenmut isn't wrong," said worldly Kasmut. "It matters that you do your duty now. Once you're married, you can do what else you like. Edjmet won't bother you."

"But I'm fourteen years old," I moaned. "I can't start thinking like that! How can I give myself to a man with bad body odour and a feeble brain?"

"Look at your father," she replied, "and ask yourself how long he has left in him. Would you prefer Edjmet on the throne, married for instance, to Esho? What would that do for *maat*?"

Then at the next audience, when I'd decided I'd finally lost my father to the silliness of old age, Thutmose was suddenly much more like himself again, upright and renewed in energy.

"We need a break," he declared. "According to the scribes the next few days are excellent for travelling. It's time to visit the north. We leave for Memphis tomorrow."

And when the Pharaoh speaks, it's done. Just like that.

When the might of the Egyptian nation puts itself to a task, there's no power on earth that can resist it. Look at the huge columns outside the temple at Karnak and imagine how they could have made the 200-mile journey from the southern quarries. It seems impossible, but by the skill of the engineers and by huge numbers of men working together, an unbearable weight becomes light work. See our armies stretched out on the plain outside the city of Thebes, rank after rank, and it's incredible that such a force could be mustered, and clear that no other army could ever be their match. As the royal barges were muscled up the Nile by the oars of burly sailors, the extra impetus of a southerly wind on the sails ensuring that we made at least 100 miles each day, I felt completely exhilarated, and completely powerful. Wasn't this the life! And I'm ashamed to say it, I began to forget Rami.

Each night a different palace by the riverbank, each night a new banquet, each night extravagant entertainment. All the way from Thebes, through Abydos and on round the endless curves to Memphis, jugglers and fire-eaters, dancers of the greatest beauty and elegance from the four corners of the world, contortionists and gymnasts, storytellers and singers, snake charmers and comedians. At times even Edjmet was impressed.

"Bravo," he shouted. "Encore! Aren't they g-g-good, A-a-a-asha?"

Each time he said my name, it came out as a sneeze. I was trying to like him better, to find a lovable feature, honestly I was. He wasn't unkind. He didn't have a wandering eye. In the open air on the deck of the barge the pong wasn't so bad…

And then as we rounded a bend on the river close to sunset on the fifth day, we caught our first glimpse of the great collection of pyramids at Giza. Behind them the sky was a kaleidoscope of colour, changing by the minute from orange to crimson-red to mauve. It was a totally awe-inspiring sight. It made you think of eternity and heaven and *everything* all at once. Nofret gripped my shoulder. I opened my mouth, but no words came out. There was nothing you *could* say, not in the face of 1,000 or more years of history.

What had those ancient Pharaohs been like? Did they think like us? Would we have even understood them?

Senenmut once told me that back then they spoke completely differently from the way we do today.

The little palace at Giza lies within a mile or two of the great pyramids. Once long ago it was a greener place, but over the years the desert has crept in around the towering stones of the old tombs and the outstretched paws of the Sphinx. The first day we were there it was impossibly, unseasonably hot. There wasn't the slightest breath of wind to take the edge off the burning sun. The heat reflected relentlessly, stiflingly off the sand. The river flowed a sluggish grey-green, and an unpleasant sour smell hung about it, drifting into the scrappy palace gardens. The humidity was affecting us all, but my father most of all. He'd recently taken to walking with a stick, but now even that was too much for him, and at dusk he was carried out on a shaded chair towards old King Khufu's pyramid with only the immediate family for company.

"Come close to me, daughter," he whispered, his voice a croak. It was shocking how in just a month he'd become so thin, the skin drawn across his face like the most delicate and fine papyrus.

"Do you see how well the stones fit together?"

"I see it, Father," I answered, looking and marvelling with him. Each stone nestled precisely on the next, without any apparent need for mortar to keep them in place.

"We wouldn't do it the same way now – perhaps our stonemasons aren't as good. But we must keep the faith that was theirs. It's a sacred trust. We must keep building – the best we can. People as well as tombs. Do you understand me?"

"I do, Father. At least I think so."

"I want you to take Edjmet as your husband. Here. Tomorrow."

My heart pounded. Secretly I'd hoped that it would never come to this, hoped even that my father would die before he asked such a thing of me. But how could I refuse him now?

"If you tell me it's what you want, I will do it."

"It's what I desire with all my heart, daughter. It will secure the kingdom. Amun will fit you two together as closely as these stones. I know he will."

And so the next morning, with the pyramids as a backdrop, before my father, Ahmose, Shushu, Senenmut and all our travelling court, with Nofret and Kasmut as my companions and witnesses, I married my half-brother, the idiot Edjmet, who at one and the same time was officially designated heir to the throne of Egypt. He giggled all day long, and a cruel smile never once left the vizier Shushu's face. To him the day's events brought final triumph a little closer, or so he thought. His puppet was a single heartbeat away from the throne of Egypt, and he was itching to start pulling the strings.

And so it proved. On that very night, my wedding night, and quietly in his sleep, close to the royal tombs of his most distant ancestors, my dear father died. I awoke to the devastating news that I'd become not only a wife, but also Queen Consort to a new King Thutmose. At least, in taking my father's name, Edjmet's first action as Pharaoh had been the right one. Or rather, Senenmut and Shushu had agreed on that one thing, if nothing else.

Book two
FLOOD

Four months later

I hope you'll forgive me. Life is so busy and it's harder than ever to find the time to write. I will have to be brief.

I'm proud that during that day and the ones that followed I believe I was everything an Egyptian queen should be. During the previous months people had kept telling me I was a grown-up and should behave like one. Now *I* knew I had to be strong, and while everyone around me was falling apart, I worked at keeping my mind clear.

Late in the afternoon I found Senenmut and Shushu with their heads together, muttering. The atmosphere suggested an argument. I didn't interrupt, but just waited for them to see I was there.

Senenmut finally noticed me and cleared his throat.

"We were just talking, Your Highness, about the arrangements for your father's body."

"Is there a problem?" I said.

Senenmut licked his lips. He seemed to be looking for the right words.

"It's all right, Senny," I said quietly. "Don't worry! Whatever it is, you won't hurt my feelings."

"It's a delicate matter, madam. And your opinion's important. When they embalmed Wadjmose's body before bringing it home, those country people didn't do a good job. The real experts are back home in Thebes. Even here in Memphis it's hard to know who to trust. So, do we temporarily try to stabilize your father's body and then move it as quickly as possible to Thebes, or should we risk the work being done here? Either way, in this heat, we have to move fast."

"My father's eternal soul is at stake," I said. "We need to take the least possible risk. The Thebes option has got to be the right one."

Shushu threw up his hands in frustration. As far as he was concerned, that was clearly the wrong answer, though for the life of me I couldn't see why. But my mother agreed with me, and Shushu was overruled.

In the afterlife, the body of the Pharaoh would be reunited with his *ba*, the spirit which flew from him at his death. So it was important that my father's mummified body should be preserved as perfectly as possible ready for that heavenly meeting. First the internal organs needed to be removed – easier in some cases than in others (brain removal is very specialized work) – and the important ones stored separately in airtight jars. Then the body needed to be dried and the new cavities packed with preservatives. Only my father's stout heart would stay in its place. For after all, what more important organ in the body is there?

A plan was made to perform the most basic surgery at once, and then start the drying process as best we could while sending messages ahead so that the embalmers in Thebes would be ready and waiting for our arrival.

Our second journey along the Nile was very different from the first. This time there was no rejoicing at each overnight stop. No conjurers. No comedians. And during the days, as we passed each settlement, the banks of the great river were lined with ordinary people silently paying their respects. All work stopped as we went by, and hour after hour on board the only sounds were of oars straining against the water, birds mewing from the reeds, and wailing groups of women, throwing sand over themselves and casting spring flowers into the water.

"They really loved him, didn't they?" said Nofret wistfully as the barges rowed past yet another squat mud-brick village.

"He looked after them," I answered, "and loved them too – in his own way. Let's hope that the new Pharaoh is half the man our father was."

The signs weren't hopeful.

I'd begun to notice how obsessive Edjmet was. For example, his figs had to be peeled in precisely the right way, from the top downwards in strips, so that not the slightest scrap of skin remained and the fruit remained perfectly formed. Nothing else would do. His new beard grew lavishly, and he was pernickety to the last hair about how much the barber cut it at each side. For *each night's sleep* he required a freshly stuffed pillow of duck down. And these were just three of a thousand things that had to be just so. If you're *that* fussy a person, there's always bound to be something wrong, and you're therefore always likely to be unhappy. My line with him was to say, "Does it really matter, Edjmet? Aren't there more important things in the world?"

But he would always answer peevishly, "Of course it matters. Things must be done in the right way."

So I would reply, "But are you sure your way *is* the right way?"

To which his retort was, absolutely seriously, "Of course. What other way is there?"

As King he was like a child with a new doll. On only the third day the peeling of the figs went wrong at dinner. The servants brought slightly blemished and bruised fruit to the table. When I say *slightly*, I mean it. I couldn't see anything wrong with them at all, but Edjmet flew into a blind rage.

"Is it *impossible* for the Pharaoh to have even the simplest thing done properly?" he suddenly screamed, scattering bowls and fruit with a sweep of his forearm. The staff were scandalized. My father had his faults, but in all his years they'd never seen him lose his temper in such a way.

It was a difficult time, of course it was. For me too! Once we were home everything suddenly changed. I was moved out of my old familiar room in the harem into the main palace, and suddenly I felt lost and alone under the gaze of all the courtiers and advisers every hour of each day. My mother Ahmose was close by, but she was walled up in her own tomb of grief. For so long she'd been the principal woman of the harem. Now overnight that role had passed to me. Without a job to do, she walked the corridors of the palace, fingering her worry beads, listless and sad. Nothing I could say was of any help.

It was soon the New Year festival, and the new Pharaoh and his consort would have to make their first public appearances. The palace was suddenly filled with people demanding Edjmet's attention. Shushu and his staff kept most of them away, but there was still much urgent business to be attended to. Things which hadn't been problems, now obviously became so. To hear people talk, the army was in chaos, arguing about pay and who should command which regiment. There were shortages of cloth and vegetables, even though the harvest had been declared excellent. The minister for the law courts fell out with the minister for trade and they were found fighting on the floor of one of the palace rooms. Edjmet couldn't remotely cope with any of it. He heard briefings and didn't understand them, or at a serious moment he'd remember a private joke and start giggling inanely. Sometimes, frustrated by his own stupidity, he'd fly into a rage, and throw whatever came to hand or kick whatever was in his way. I worried that one day a kick would come in my direction, but strangely, he never turned his anger on me. Instead he'd come and cry on my shoulder when he'd just thrown a tantrum, saying "I-I-I don't know why I do it, A-a-a-asha. I'm so sorry. Really I am. I'm such a b-b-bad person…"

And I'd cuddle him and tell him it was all right – more like a mother to him than a wife.

Senenmut kept me up to date.

"There's a problem with the stonemasons at Karnak, Your Highness," he whispered one day during one of our morning chats. "They're not being paid, and they're beginning to grumble. If we're not careful, the trouble will spread."

"Doesn't Shushu have it under control?" I asked.

"I think he may be part of the problem."

"How come?"

"He never wanted the projects that your father commissioned up there. He'd like to see the stonemasons laid off, and a stop put to what he thinks is a waste of money. What Shushu doesn't understand is that with the stonemasons it's 'one out, all out'. Cross them on this one, and building work right across Thebes might grind to a halt. Including work on your father's funeral temple. And that would be a disaster!"

"What can I do?"

"Nothing at present. But you may have to try to get Edjmet to put his foot down."

I said nothing but thought to myself, "*And how exactly do I do that?*"

The days ticked down to my father's funeral, and I was becoming more miserable and dull with each one.

"You know what's wrong with you," said Nofret, as we sat in the harem one afternoon.

"No. What?"

"You need a run! That would make you feel better."

I sat up a little straighter.

"Wouldn't it be nice?" I said, and even the thought brightened the day. Then I remembered who I was. "But I can't," I moaned. "A queen can't go prancing about like a silly girl."

"I thought a queen could do anything she liked," said Nofret. "And anyway, six months ago, this queen *was* a silly girl. She doesn't look much different to me now from how she did then."

I remembered my father's words about getting the women to exercise. I stood up, rolled my shoulders a few times and stretched.

"Well, that's telling me!" I said, taking deep breaths. "But you're quite right, Nofret. A run would do me good. It would do us *all* good."

"You don't mean..." said my sister, horrified. Remember – she hadn't run anywhere in years!

"I do. Let's go and change. Right now. No, on second thoughts, before you do that, go and invite all the harem women under the age of 30 to join the Queen for a spot of jogging. Nothing too energetic. Tell them there's nothing like it for toning their underworked muscles. It'll make them even more beautiful. And that includes Esho!"

And so with Senbi and two other trusted guards keeping prying eyes away, the Harem Running Club had its first meeting up in the roof garden.

But someone couldn't keep a secret. Probably Esho.

"I don't approve, Your Highness," growled Shushu. "Whoever heard of such a thing? If I may advise, leave the menfolk to bodybuilding, and devote yourself to the proper activities of a wife. The King's household is a disgrace. He tells me his food is never the way he wishes it. And while we're about it, isn't it time you considered the question of children?"

The cheek of the man. I looked at him coldly.

"Thank you for your advice, vizier Shushu. As always, I'll consider carefully what you have to say."

Later that evening Edjmet added his disapproval.

"I don't think you should be running around like that, A-A-A-asha. Shushu doesn't like it."

"Shushu doesn't like figs either," I replied, which was true. He couldn't stand the taste of them. "It doesn't stop you eating them, does it?"

That was the thing with Edjmet. Teasing him was no fun at all. Even the simplest argument completely floored him.

So every other day, all the women and girls jogged for the sake of their health. I felt much better. It wasn't sky-skimming – and how I longed for those days – but it was better than nothing.

Ten days before the funeral I had a surprise. In the line of people waiting to see me in the palace's throne room was Akhpet.

"Your Highness," he said, with a deep bow.

"How good to see you again," I said, smiling. "What are you doing here?"

"The statue of your father," he answered. "The one he commissioned."

I looked blank. "I know nothing about it, Akhpet," I said. "You'll have to enlighten me."

"It was last year, Your Highness. He said he wanted one made for the temple at Karnak, to honour Amun. So now I've had it brought to the lobby, awaiting your mother's approval. And yours, of course!"

I followed him through into the hallway, and there, standing on a small sledge, was the statue. The first glimpse of it jolted tears to my eyes. In every important detail, Akhpet and his colleagues had conjured up the absolute likeness of my father: the gaze, the slight forward inclination of the head, the high intelligent brow. More than that, they'd somehow captured Thutmose's *ka* in all its kindliness and patience. At that moment it just so happened that my mother walked by, and when she saw it she too was immediately overwhelmed. We stood there holding on to each other, sad and happy at the same time.

"How is … how is Rami?" I asked eventually, when we'd recovered our dignity. I felt almost ashamed to ask. At the same time I felt disloyal both to Edjmet, since I was after all his wife, and to Rami, for forgetting him.

Akhpet beamed. "He's well, Your Highness. The best son a father could have. Grown as tall as a tree."

With a lump in my throat I said I was very glad, and that he must take my best wishes to him.

My mother asked if we could keep the statue with us for a little while.

"Of course," said Akhpet. "Why don't I come back in a few days and collect it? That still gives me time for some last finishing touches – before the funeral. The vizier has suggested that as the right time for its installation at Karnak."

I felt the anger rise inside me. Shushu! Always interfering!

Always with his hands on our family's most precious possessions. Would I have to live with his interference for the rest of my days?

To be truthful, amid all the things that had to be done it slipped my mind that Akhpet was due to return, and so three days later I was caught by surprise when a concerned-looking Senenmut told me of his arrival in the palace compound.

"There's something you should know," he said drawing me to one side. "The man's in pieces. The way he is now, someone else will need to deal with your father's statue. It's your friend Rami. He was bitten by a snake this morning. They think he may die."

I gave a shriek of despair. "Oh, Senny. Where is he? I've got to go and see him," I cried. "Now!"

"Steady on, Your Highness," said Senenmut in measured tones. "Akhpet's brought him here, in the hope that something can be done. All the local doctors were doing was chanting spells and making him vomit."

"*Is* there anything we can do to help?"

Senenmut looked doubtful.

"It depends on the kind of snake – and how long the venom's been in his system. But if Your Highness allows it, we can get the court physicians to take a look…"

"Of course I allow it," I said. "Whatever's possible. Make it happen, Senenmut. This is so important to me."

Here in the palace we're protected from so much that ordinary people have to cope with. For those who work in the fields, being bitten by poisonous snakes is a daily risk. I waited anxiously for news, pacing the corridors, wringing my hands. It was an hour before Senenmut returned to give me a report.

"Good news, Your Highness. Your friend's still very unwell, but there's a chance. They've removed the poison, and opened his throat to help him breathe. However, he still has a fever. They say tonight will be critical."

That evening I went to the shrine of Hathor, made a sacrifice and begged for her help. And I asked Senbi to take Rami one of my most treasured possessions: an amulet in the shape of a silver scarab beetle which my father had given me.

"Slip it round his neck, Senbi. It will keep him safe!"

In the morning Akhpet himself came to see me. He was gaunt and grey from lack of sleep, but now there was a wan smile on his face. "How can I thank you enough?" he said. "Rami opened his eyes this morning, and was well enough to take a little broth. The doctors believe he will live. Praise be to the goddess Hathor!"

I saw Rami twice in the next days. He was still weak and could do little more than raise his arm in greeting. I patted his hand, and told him not to try to speak. Instead Akhpet spoke for him. "Rami promises you," he said passionately, "and so do I – we will find a way to repay you for your kindness."

As the days counted down to my father's funeral, a great weight seemed to be pressing on us. The arrangements were complicated and elaborate. Dignitaries from abroad, and the great and good from every corner of Egypt thronged the centre of Thebes. At the time of his death, my father's funeral temple on the west bank of the river had still been a building site. It had been touch and go to make it ready for the day of the ceremony. Hundreds of labourers had worked without a break to at least give the impression that everything was the way it should be. There was to be a great public event in the heart of the city before we moved across the river for the most solemn moments of the ritual.

Is there really life after death? Some of our poets poke fun at the idea, and yet we Egyptians give so much time to our religion, it sometimes seems as if we're preparing to die the whole of our lives. What I do know is that Rami's return from the brink of death had lifted my spirits. A prayer had been answered, and that was what gave me the strength to say my goodbyes to my father, in the belief that one day I'd see him again.

The day itself passed surprisingly quickly and easily. I spent so much energy making sure Edjmet behaved himself, and supporting my mother, that there wasn't any opportunity to worry about what *I* was feeling. There were hundreds of people to greet. A thousand words of sympathy to receive. But I'll never forget those late afternoon hours, when we'd travelled across the Nile and walked in procession up to Thutmose's temple. Ear-piercing trumpets and clattering drums had made it impossible to think in Thebes. Here on the west bank, amid stately dancing to the gentle sounds of a flute and with the distant wailing of the official mourners expressing the grief we felt, there was time to remember. Birds of prey wheeled in the sky as we watched the great play of the "opening of the mouth" as it was performed in front of my father's sarcophagus. Around him lay his most precious possessions. His hunting spears. His sceptre of office. A harp. His favourite food laid out on the best tableware. His finest clothes. And, prominently displayed, Akhpet's statue.

"I thought the statue was going to Karnak," I whispered to Senenmut.

"A last-minute change of plan, it seems, madam," he replied. "The vizier's orders…"

I began to protest, but he cut me off. "With respect, Your Highness, it's not something I can do anything about. You'll have to raise the matter yourself with the vizier or your husband…"

Which was to say, there was nothing that could be done at all. For whatever reason, the lovely statue was destined never to see the light of day again. Shortly it would be walled up with my father's body in his tomb. Without it, how would I remember what my father looked like, his smile, his honest, piercing eyes?

As the sun began to set, the ground was purified with water, candles of incense were lit, and members of the royal household donned head-dresses and masks as the battle in which the god Horus avenged his father Osiris was re-enacted. Nofret played the part of Queen Isis. Senbi was Horus. The priests made sacrifices of two bulls, one for the north kingdom and one for the south. The heart of the southern bull was removed and offered to my father where he lay in his open coffin. The high priest moved forward and touched my father's lips gently with his staff, saying, "Thy mouth was shut, but now have I established thy mouth and teeth. I open thy mouth. I open thy two eyes. And now thou shalt walk and speak a second time. Thy body will fly to be with the company of the gods in heaven. Thou art reborn. Thou art young again. Thou art reborn. Thou art young again…"

And with these words, and in total silence, my father was carried away from our sight along the funeral route to his tomb with all that would accompany him to the other world, wherever that may be. May his *ba* rest in peace and be reunited with his body in heaven.

I'd thought Edjmet was still at my side, but while I was concentrating on the ritual he must have wandered off. Turning my head to look for him, I saw him at one side of the gathering, deep in conversation with Shushu. The vizier was pointing with one hand, and explaining something animatedly, his other hand cupped so that no one else could hear.

"Watch your back, daughter of one Pharaoh and queen of a second!" said Kasmut, sidling up to me. "Shushu's ambition knows no bounds. There's nothing so dangerous as a man who believes his country needs what only he can give."

That night, as we crossed the Nile back to the palace, the wind was from the south and there was a great muddiness in the water. The boat rocked and rolled in the current. The flood was beginning. And beginning early.

Book two
PLANTING

Four months later

Time has moved on so quickly. Already these events seem a long way in the past. As I come to the climax of my story, I hope that what I write will be true, accurate and fair. I want you to think well of me.

As far as I can remember, some days after the funeral I was sitting with Ahmose beside one of the harem garden's sweet-smelling frankincense trees.

"What a relief the funeral's over and done with!" she sighed. "Does that sound awful?"

"I feel exactly the same," I said, folding my arm in hers. "I miss Dad badly, but now we've got to get on with the rest of our lives."

"And how *is* Edjmet?"

"Who?"

And we both laughed.

Edjmet was shrinking into himself and his room. Whenever he could, he shied away from anything that resembled work, preferring to leave things to Shushu or –

when the vizier was out of the palace on business – to me and Senenmut. Whatever the problem, it always seemed too hard for Edjmet's poor little brain. Shushu was never shy of encouraging his laziness.

"You look pale today, Your Highness," he would say, with apparent sympathy. "How are you feeling?"

"Now you come to mention it," Edjmet would reply, looking relieved, "I-I-I'm not myself at all. I think perhaps I should take it easy, if that's all right with you."

Which of course it always was. Increasingly, Shushu was becoming the voice of Pharaoh.

"What the King thinks is…" or "What His Majesty wants…" was a way he began many sentences, which often left me wondering, *Really? Then how come he's never said so to me?*

Shushu even tried it on with Senenmut.

"His Majesty wants a written account of how senior staff spend their time," Shushu remarked one day in my hearing. "Including you, Senenmut. The King's concerned too many people are wasting their days away."

In fact Shushu wasn't wrong about *that*. Too many in the court were taking their lead from Edjmet. Suddenly there was a lot of unexplained "sickness". People stood gossiping when they should have been working. Getting anything done was becoming impossible.

"Well, if that's the case…" Senenmut said, genuinely puzzled, "it's odd he's not said anything to me…"

"Why do you always have to question everything I say?" Shushu growled.

"I'm sorry if you think I do, Shushu," said Senenmut, raising his voice a little. "I can see there's a problem, but personally the last thing I need is more paperwork."

"Oh forget it!" said Shushu crossly. "If the kingdom goes to rack and ruin, what do I care?"

"And the truth of it is, he *doesn't* care, either," said a furious Senenmut to me later, "because if the kingdom starts to fall apart, he'll claim it's all Edjmet's fault, and there's only one man who can put things right – and I think we know who that is!"

Around the harem, my training sessions had suddenly become distinctly fashionable. Interestingly, you were now an "in" person if you could show a bit of running style and "out" if you were a flat-footed wobbler. With Senbi's help I set up an obstacle course around the roofs, to make things a bit more interesting – nothing dangerous, just the odd wall to vault here, a long jump there.

"Just imagine it's a gap between two buildings," I shouted. "One slip, and you'll break your neck. Go on, Esho, make the most of those legs of yours!"

Daringly, I introduced them to throwing. Quoits weren't

a problem, but when I suggested spears, there were mixed opinions.

"I could never do that," said one. "Not with my build. Too much to get in the way!"

"No, not very ladylike," muttered another.

"Fun, though," I answered. "And why should men be the only ones to have some of *that*?"

It was Nofret's suggestion to have a morning of competitive games. Even the women who never joined in turned up to watch. Including my mother! The day was a great success, on the whole. I presided over the event, and didn't take part myself – I was still much faster than anyone else, and had no particular wish to show people up. But towards the end I did run the obstacle course on my own against Nofret's count, just the way we'd done in the old days.

I have to admit, it had all become rather rowdy, with cheers and jeers, and the kind of bawdy language men think women don't know. The noise must have reached Shushu's office, because he suddenly appeared during the javelin – the morning's last event. To make matters worse, Esho was the one throwing. She has a powerful arm but no sense of direction. Her spear veered away on a path which took it unfortunately close to the vizier's nose. Esho's hand went to her mouth.

"What in the name of Thoth is going on here?" he spluttered, as the spear clattered on to a marble staircase behind him. "This is an outrage. Who exactly do you think you are? This is no way for women to behave. Get yourselves back inside immediately. The King will have something to say about this."

I couldn't help myself. I stood up and confronted him. The other women fell silent.

"You have no rights over the harem, Shushu," I said. "I'm the boss here. What we do to entertain ourselves is our business, not yours. Perhaps Egypt needs strong women since its men are so weak and self-serving. Look to your own fitness and leave us to make ourselves beautiful in the ways we choose."

"I will not trade arguments with you here, madam," he said icily, "but I will talk with you later." And he turned on his heel and strode off.

I left it a few minutes, and then went to find him.

"Listen to me, Shushu…" I started, unwisely, still on fire with anger.

"No. You listen to me," he hissed. "As yet, you're fourteen years old. *Fourteen!* You've done nothing. You know nothing. You may be the daughter of a king, and married to another. You may be 'boss' in the safety of the harem. But remember what I once said to you and be very afraid. With your father gone there's no one to protect you, not even your champion Senenmut, and there are a thousand ways in which misfortune could befall you, from food poisoning to, yes, *a wayward spear*. Think of your brother Wadjmose and behave, young woman. Or prepare to shortly follow him and your father to the grave."

There was a frightening power in his eyes, and cowed by the violence and outrageousness of his words, I began to cry. Later, on my own again, I hated myself for being so weak. What kind of a leader was I?

I told Senenmut what had happened. He pursed his lips. "Perhaps it wasn't the wisest thing to have done," he murmured.

"Why shouldn't we have some fun if we want to?" I pouted.

"Well now you *sound* like a fourteen-year-old girl, and not the Queen. You *should* remember who you are. I don't say you were wrong to have the competition. Just that you weren't being very clever to take on Shushu like that in public. Sometimes, you know, you must retreat if you want to win a battle."

I was stung by his rebuke, and said miserably, "So we must stop our running and throwing?"

"No. That's not what I mean at all. Quite the contrary. Just don't draw attention to it. And of course, there'd be no harm in apologizing to Shushu for speaking out of turn."

"*Apologize?*"

"Would that be so bad? Soft words turn away anger. And in my opinion, if we give Shushu enough rope, sooner or later he'll hang himself. Showing how reasonable you are now may come in useful later."

I did as Senenmut had suggested, swallowed my pride, and that evening went to find Shushu. The vizier looked at me suspiciously as I bowed to him, the very picture of a meek submissive girl.

"Yes, well, thank you," he muttered. Caught off guard, he obviously didn't know quite what to say but added in his usual pompous manner, "Always remember, madam, the dignity of Pharaoh's court is the most important thing."

However, as the events of a few days later showed, dignity wasn't the first word which necessarily came to mind in Pharaoh's court.

Strong drink had become another easy way for Edjmet to escape from real life. Agreed, alcohol is a necessary part of our lives. The weak beer we drink with our meals is the safest drink in our hot country where the water can't be trusted, and we drink a lot of it. But it should be a point of honour for any Egyptian of standing, and royalty above all, never, ever to show themselves drunk. But some days, even by the time the sun was at its peak, I could tell from Edjmet's breath and the way he held on to the furniture as he rolled around the palace that he was tipsy. There are liquors you can buy, distilled from Amun knows what, which will rob you of the use of your legs in half an hour. Clearly Edjmet had begun to find the courage they gave him useful.

This one particular morning, he wandered across the room and slumped on to his throne. His speech was slurred.

"Worra you got for me this morning, Shushy?" he asked.

I could see some of the servants turning away to suppress their giggles. You did not, you just did not, ever address the vizier in such a familiar way. Whoever you were.

Shushu frowned, and looked disdainfully at his king.

"Is Your Majesty feeling quite well today?"

"Fine, old boy. N-n-never … never felt better. How are y-y-you?"

"Your Majesty need have no concern."

Edjmet was sufficiently emboldened by the drink to attempt an impression of Shushu.

"H-h-his Majesty need have no concern, eh, Shushy? B-b-but I'm Pharaoh, aren't I? And Ph-ph-pharaoh should have concern for all his subjects, shouldn't he?"

"Indeed he should, sir."

"So come on, tell me. How *are* you? Everything in working order? B-b-bowels f-f-fully functioning? T-t-tongue clean?"

And for some reason, Edjmet, having first laughed crazily to himself, started barking like a dog. His impression of Mek was rather better than his impression of Shushu.

The vizier shook his head, rolled his eyes and looked across at me for assistance. I shrugged my shoulders. When Edjmet had left his bedchamber two hours earlier he'd seemed his normal idiot self, but at least sober.

Shushu said forcefully, "I really think Your Majesty should go back to bed, until you're feeling less…" He searched for the right word. "…tired!"

Edjmet snapped back petulantly, "I told you, I'm perfectly fit for work. Tell me who's f-f-first on the list, and let's be qu-qu-quick about it. Haven't got all day." And he began to whistle tunelessly.

"Very well," said Shushu who, mystified, apparently couldn't think what to do next. For once I felt a twinge of sympathy for him.

Two men were brought in. Apparently they'd worked in the palace kitchens for some years, but had been caught pilfering small quantities of food to take home to their families. The face of one of them rang a vague bell: the other I didn't know at all. Although they worked in the palace they wouldn't have been paid particularly well. And very probably they had large families and many dependents to feed.

"A trivial matter, Your Majesty," Shushu whispered in Edjmet's ear. "I'd recommend a short spell of hard labour, and eventual reinstatement in their posts. The one who's a cook is rather good at his job, so the head steward tells me."

Edjmet's head lolled on to the side of the throne. His eyes were wild and staring – I'd never seen him look that way before. I suddenly felt a flash of fear for the two men.

"That's what *you'd* recommend, is it Shushy? Well, I

don't think it's what *I'd* r-r-recommend." He sat upright and stabbed a finger towards the vizier. "I … th-th-think … you're … g-g-going … soft."

He fell backwards to his original position, and then, his face contorting, he shouted at the top of his voice. "Guards!" No one moved. Edjmet shouted a second time. When still nothing happened, and with embarrassment now showing on everyone's face, he tried a third time. This time the order was simply screamed out. There was a confused hubbub in the corridor and three members of the palace guard finally presented themselves. The two men looked terrified, their eyes appealing to Shushu, to me, to Senenmut, to anyone to help them.

"T-t-take these men away and c-c-cut off their heads," said Edjmet.

"Your Majesty…" intervened Shushu, genuinely appalled.

"Don't interrupt, Shushy. Pharaoh's talking. We'll have no f-f-falling s-s-standards in my c-c-court. Do you hear me? What are you waiting for, guards? Do as I tell you. Now! Unless you want the same to h-h-happen to y-y-you."

The astonished guards looked across to Shushu for confirmation. Reluctantly, he nodded his head.

I mouthed at Senenmut, "They *can't*…" but he shook his head as if to say, "Not now!" and the men were bundled from the room, still shouting their protests. Senenmut came to my side and whispered, "Leave it. There's nothing we can do."

"Now w-w-what's nexsht?" asked Edjmet.

"No more business, Your Majesty. Not today," said Shushu firmly.

"Sh-sh-shame," the King said, clearly disappointed. "I w-w-was jusht g-g-getting into my sh-sh-shtride."

After Edjmet had been carried away to sleep off the morning's drinking, Senenmut said to Shushu, "It's barbaric! Surely we can't allow this?"

"For once I agree," said the vizier. "But unfortunately, what the Pharaoh wants, he must get. That's the way it works. As you should know."

Senenmut's eyes narrowed. These were weasel words. Either way Shushu knew he would win. If Edjmet insisted, he could claim the new Pharaoh was unstable. On the other hand, if he could be seen to dissuade him from such cruelty, he'd claim the credit for being the only one who could influence Edjmet towards mercy.

"Shouldn't we wait until Edjmet wakes up," I suggested, "and see what he thinks then?"

When Edjmet did wake up, some time later in the afternoon, he had a very sore head and couldn't remember much of what had happened that morning. Unfortunately, everyone else's memory was in fine shape. The Pharaoh's bad behaviour was the talk of the palace for days afterwards. It hurt me to catch sight of people making fun of him behind his back, imitating his drunken walk, knocking back imaginary cups of beer and pretending to fall over.

Fortunately the palace guards showed common sense and delayed the two men's execution until Shushu had confirmed it. The men were freed and told to make themselves scarce, happy to escape with their lives. The real damage had been done to Edjmet's reputation.

"There's a lot of discontent," Senenmut said to me later in a quiet and confidential voice. "Particularly among the army and the temple priests. They think Edjmet and Shushu are a bad combination. It's very serious, Asha. This could put us all in danger. If the army decided to move on the palace, we'd all be for the chop, however blameless you and I might be. Isn't there anything you can do with the King?"

"I'll try," I said. "Of course, I will. But I don't think he listens to me."

What was needed was for Edjmet to apologize, to show some backbone, and act more like a Pharaoh. Instead all he could do was gibber, and promise not to do it again. He was ashamed of himself, but it changed nothing.

So when the stonemasons at Karnak did as they'd threatened and finally downed tools, and when their colleagues elsewhere in the city came out on strike in sympathy, it was obvious Edjmet was going to be no help whatsoever. The foreman of the temple workers and three of his colleagues stood before us, sullen and stroppy.

"We ain't doin' it no more," the foreman said. "We've had enough."

"What's the problem?" asked Shushu smoothly.

"We ain't been paid for Amun knows how long. It's always 'promises, promises'. 'Five days' time', they tells us and then five days' time never arrives. So that's it. You want to try it, mate. Out there in the sun every day, twelve hours at a go, shifting bloomin' great blocks of stone around."

"I can't think how that can have happened," Shushu lied. "Most regrettable!" He was the one, of course, behind their lack of wages.

"Well, we wants you to sort it, or there won't be nothing else built across this city until you do!"

"Hmm. Leave it with me. Go back to work, and in due course someone will come and tell you what's been done."

"Begging your pardon, *sir*, but we ain't goin' nowhere. We'll just sit down where we are and wait till you've got the payment organized, won't we lads?"

And they did exactly that, squatting on the floor in front of the raised dais where the King would have been sitting on his throne – if he could have been bothered.

"What should we do?" Shushu asked Senenmut. I could read his mind. It was a tricky situation: Shushu wanted to be able to spread the blame around. "Of course, I'd like to throw them to the crocodiles, but…"

"But there'd be a riot," Senenmut finished for him. "Quite!"

All day the stonemasons sat there, making the place look untidy, though it was obvious a need for food or the toilet would get the better of them eventually. Even when it did and they stomped their way loudly out of the palace that evening the problem still remained. No building work was being done, and there were rumours of the discontent spreading to other tradespeople in the city.

"Oh, pay them, Shushu," said Senenmut tetchily. "And if you really don't want that work to continue at Karnak, just get the Pharaoh's agreement for it to be stopped. Different Pharaohs have different ideas about public works. It's always been that way. It always will be. The people of Thebes will accept it. But if you keep tweaking the lion's tail eventually it will turn round and bite you."

"I refuse to be ordered about by a bunch of louts," said the vizier. "I'll show them who's boss!" It was always the same. If Senenmut said "white", Shushu would plump for "black".

So the next day there was a full-scale riot. An angry crowd tried to storm the palace gates. We were safe inside, but could still hear the din. Even at 300 paces it was terrifying. Luckily for us, the army stayed loyal to the Pharaoh, and the labourers with their staffs and fists were no match for the discipline and spears of the soldiers. But 30 men died that day. Thirty bodies, laid out on the paving in front of the palace. A dreadful, unheard-of disaster. I thought about Akhpet and Rami and hoped they'd been far away from the danger.

The army's commander-in-chief, Hor, sought an audience with Edjmet. What he actually got was an interview with Shushu, and if Senenmut hadn't insisted that I be there too, it would have been one to one. It was obvious to both of us. The vizier was positioning himself for power.

"What can I do?" Shushu said to Hor, spreading his hands. "I've said to the Pharaoh, more than once, that if he wants to stop building at Karnak, he should pay the men and then lay them off. But he won't hear of it. He just refuses to release the pay rations."

As a piece of barefaced cheek it took the breath away. I couldn't resist the temptation.

"Vizier Shushu, I thought that was *your* opinion. Not the Pharaoh's!"

Shushu turned and fixed his glare on me. "No, Your Highness, you're quite mistaken."

Hor looked confused. "Whatever's the case, I have to advise you, *all* of you, that the army won't stand by idly for ever," he said. "If His Majesty can't be trusted to rule properly, we shall have to find someone who can. You understand me, Shushu?"

"I completely agree," said the vizier smoothly. "In fact I'm sure you and I would agree about most matters to do with government. I will always stand at the service of my country. You may depend on that!"

When Rami turned up at the palace the next day, at first it was a lovely surprise – and a relief. His father was right. He seemed to have grown rapidly since I'd last seen him, and was now easily two handspans taller than me. Did viper venom have some effect the doctors didn't know about? He laughed. And said I looked tired.

"Thanks," I said sarcastically. "Is that any way to address your Queen? Although of course, you're quite right. I am."

And without being disloyal, I explained how difficult life sometimes was at court. His face clouded.

"What I'm about to tell you won't make you feel any better," he said. "I've come on behalf of my father." He blushed. "And, of course, because it's good to see you again…"

"You never need an excuse," I said. "You can come here whenever you want."

"But the King … your husband…?"

"Is *only* my husband. Not my whole life. I think I should be permitted friends, don't you?"

Rami looked puzzled, and uncertain. He hopped from foot to foot.

"What I have to say will affect him too … and Asha, you must know how much I'm risking by telling you this…"

"Well, go on. Don't stop now. You know you can trust me. Don't leave me in suspense!"

"Akhpet dared not come here himself, not since the stonemasons' dispute, but it's come to his ears that a major robbery is planned at your father's tomb. The people behind it aren't amateurs. Word is that the highest people at court are involved."

Nothing surprised me these days. "And who's the source of the information?" I asked carefully.

"Djeser. One of my father's oldest friends – himself a very good artist. Very nearly as good as my father, and with the highest level of security clearance. He was working on the room where your father was buried even after your father's sarcophagus had finally been placed there. A man he knew by sight visited him and promised him riches so great that he'd never have to work again *if* he would only explain how to break into your father Thutmose's tomb. To cut a long story short, Djeser pretended to go along with the plot. He told them that it might be possible, by forcing a way in through the walls from the next-door tomb – which he believes is still empty. By his own admission he was tempted to join the robbers, but in the end he talked to my father, who persuaded

him the information must be passed on. And so you see –
that's why I'm here."

"And when he said the plot involved the 'highest people at
court', who did Djeser mean?"

"He didn't know. Or wouldn't tell."

"And has he let the criminals know he's not going to
co-operate?"

"I shouldn't think so. My father and Djeser had their
conversation only yesterday evening. I came as soon as I
safely could after that."

"Right," I said. "Don't go away. Let's get you a drink while
I work this out."

The problem with plots and conspiracies is that you start
doubting who you can trust. *The highest people at court.*
My mind of course immediately went to Shushu. He clearly
craved power. And I knew at first hand how his mind worked.
If my father's most treasured possessions came under his
control, maybe for him this would be the last confirming sign
from the gods that he really was the chosen one, the man to
lead Egypt forward. But was he the only suspect? My heart
sank. It *could* even be Senenmut, for all I knew. Could I even
risk taking him into my confidence? I wasn't certain. But did
I have a choice?

I sent a message to Kasmut. She'd know what to do. She
came at once. "Senenmut?" she said incredulously.

"Ssh. Keep your voice down!"

"Senenmut?" she whispered again. "I don't believe *that* for a moment. Your imagination's running away with you, Asha. But if you're worried, here's what you should do. Talk to Commander Hor, and see what he thinks."

"Can we trust *him*?"

Kasmut tapped her nose.

"No problem. He and I ... let's just say, we go back a long way... You could trust the commander with your life. His word really is his bond."

My aunt was a constant surprise to me. And she certainly had the commander's ear. He was there within the hour.

While Hor questioned Rami in the harem garden, I kept Senenmut out of their way, distracting him with silly conversation about Edjmet's latest foolishness – he'd developed a sudden phobia about mice, and wouldn't come out of his room. Kasmut sat in on Rami's interrogation, apparently very glad of the excuse to spend some time close to her old flame. Later, I joined them to see what Hor thought should be done.

"Your Highness," he bowed. "Your father would be proud of you. What quick thinking on your part! And your aunt's, of course."

Kasmut simpered. She was positively gooey. Maybe this thing for the general wasn't quite so far in the past!

"...And well done to this young man, too. Now. What I think we should do, given the, um ... *sensitivities* ... of the matter, is to encourage the artist Djeser to string the robbers along and see if we can't catch them in the act. Rami, do you know if there's been mention of a time for the robbery?"

"According to my father, Djeser seemed to think the next rest day was likely, sir."

"Which gives us five days to get organized. That's sufficient, I think. Leave it to me, Your Highness. I'll detail a guard to accompany young Rami here back to his father. Then they can pick up Djeser and brief him as to what we need him to do."

"There's one other thing, commander," I said. "I have a very personal interest in this – after all it's my beloved father's tomb they're intending to rob. I want to be there when you catch them. I want to know who's to blame and I want to see them suffer."

Hor looked doubtful. "There are some matters best left to the military, ma'am. Think of the responsibility your idea would place on me. What if anything were to happen to you?"

I said nothing. Just looked at him steadily.

"Remember the oracle, Hor," breathed Kasmut, her fingers resting lightly on his arm. "This is no ordinary child. She's your queen. And the hand of Amun is on her."

He melted at her touch, and yielded, with a little bow.

"So for heaven's sake don't get yourself killed!" said Kasmut later. "Stay out of the army's way, and let them do their job!"

Over the next couple of days it was hard to keep pulling the wool over Senenmut's eyes.

"Is anything the matter?" he said, frowning. It must have been obvious there was. I was doing my impression of a cat on hot stones, unable to settle to anything.

"Only Edjmet," I answered, and he looked at me askance, as if he knew I wasn't telling the truth. Apart from anything else, I was finding it hard to sleep at night, imagining all kinds of dreadful things. What if, for instance, there were other plots about which we knew nothing, and Senenmut or Shushu or someone else planned to murder me and Edjmet in our beds one night? True, Edjmet was an idiot, and not the man I'd have chosen to marry, but he didn't deserve a short life and a cruel death. Nor did I.

Hor updated me on his plans.

"What we've learned, Your Highness, is that the robbers have bribed one of the priests at your father's temple. He will let them into a tomb which is situated next door to your father's. Apparently this priest has been supervizing its construction. It's said he knows every inch of its layout, and its relation to the tombs which surround it. Once they've forced their way through the walls, the keys Djeser holds will allow the robbers access to the chambers of your father's tomb and all its treasures. So, we'll wait until the robbers are underground and there's no way out. Then we'll strike."

"But will they give us the name of the ringleader?"

Hor smiled grimly. "Once we've got them, they'll talk. They'll sing like birds. If they know what's good for them."

The way he spoke, I didn't doubt it.

On the day before the raid, as far as Senenmut was to know, it had been hurriedly arranged that once again I'd visit the west bank with Kasmut to spend time at the temples there, just as we'd done on the previous occasion. The story was that I was weighed down by grief (this would also account for my bad moods during recent days) and wanted to lighten the load by being close to my father for a few short hours.

"Are you sure you wouldn't like me to come too, Asha?" Senenmut asked.

"No, no, I'll be fine," I answered, trying to sound relaxed. "I'm sure you've got lots to do here."

"Yes, of course, madam. As always, there's much to attend to."

His words were innocent enough, but by now I was seeing shadows everywhere. I'd halfway convinced myself that even this was code for skullduggery of some kind.

Hor had told us we should take the ferry as early as possible in the morning, and to avoid arousing suspicion should make our way to the site of my father's tomb for an hour while it was still relatively cool, before retiring to the temples nearer the river during the afternoon. He'd send men to collect me at nightfall, and then with the soldiers we'd await the arrival of the criminals, which Djeser said would be shortly after midnight.

Everything went to plan. At my father's temple I found it hard to look the priests in the eye, remembering one of them was guilty of high treason, but I steeled myself to be a good actor, and greeted them all as warmly as I could.

"I'm so sorry to arrive at such short notice," I said. "It'll help me so much to spend a little time here."

When they were out of earshot, Kasmut whispered to me, "What an accomplished liar you've become, Asha!"

"It seems to be one of the skills required of a queen," I answered wryly. "I see my mum in a different light these days."

"Your father's steadiness made such things quite unnecessary," sighed Kasmut. "He was a good man, you know."

And we fell into silence, remembering him.

Later, after a long siesta, two polite but grim-faced soldiers collected me as the first diamond stars began to show against the cloth of the blue-black sky. They walked me in silence around the Valley and up the hillside behind my father's tomb. I was settled down with a blanket to keep me warm, and slowly began to realize that a number of what at first seemed to be boulders were really Hor's men, huddled up in their own cloaks but poised to surge down towards the tomb entrances when the moment came.

The hours ticked away. The moon rose high above us, and I started to feel very cold, wishing I'd let Hor do what was necessary without me. Perhaps the intelligence had been wrong anyway and no robbers were going to show! But then came the vague scraping of footfalls and a murmur of conversation somewhere down below, the effort of men shifting heavy rocks, the creak of a door being opened, shallow shafts of lamplight briefly cast across the ground.

I saw Hor stealthily rise to his feet and hold a signalling hand aloft, only to drop it an instant later and send a score of men scurrying down the hillside to disappear like rabbits into a hole that had newly appeared. There was the muffled sound of men being surprised, an obvious brief but fierce struggle, and then the captain of the guard was shouting up, "All secure, sir."

"How many taken?"

"Five in all."

"Let's see 'em, then…"

And five frightened, confused men were thrown to the ground in front of us.

"You can let *him* go," commanded Hor, before turning to explain. "That's Djeser, ma'am."

He walked up to the other four, who were now pulled to their feet, the arms of each pinned by two soldiers.

"Vermin," he snarled. "You thought to line your own pockets at the expense of your country's honour and safety. Scum! Filth!"

And going down the line he brought his hand sharply back and forth across the face of each in turn.

"Now, tell us who put you up to this. Come on. Be quick about it. It's obvious you're not clever enough to have thought it up on your own. Speak, or be sure, you'll tell us later. After a lot of pain and trouble."

At first there was a silence broken only by the prisoners' groans as the soldiers twisted their arms higher and higher up their backs. I felt my heart beating faster. The moment of truth would soon arrive. Who was behind the plot?

"Very well!" said Hor, and pointed at the shortest of the men. His eyes were huge, white with terror in the moonlight. Two soldiers took him to one side. I'm glad I didn't see what they did, but I can hear the man's screams even now. A terrible sound, more like the screech of some carrion bird than the cry of a human, echoed and re-echoed from the stones on the crags around us.

"*Now* would anyone like to share with us what they know? To spare further unpleasantness…"

There was a further silence. Hor nodded at the soldiers again and they moved to take a second man; by his clothes the priest whose information had made the attempted theft possible. He dropped to his knees and put his hands together in a desperate plea for mercy.

"I'll tell you," he said. "I'll tell you…"

Time seemed to stop for me.

"You should talk to Shushu," he said. "Shushu the vizier."

Book two
HARVEST

I'm having to learn that, even in the best-run operations, mistakes sometimes occur. Sensible plans can go wrong. The unexpected happens.

Perhaps we shouldn't have waited until dawn before returning to the palace for Shushu's arrest, but there were good reasons for delaying. Apart from anything else the river crossing is never to be taken for granted. The Nile may be our friend and life-giver but sometimes the god Hapi takes from us too. People are swept away when the river is swollen. And beneath the waters, in amongst the reeds, lies the land of the crocodiles. Go there carelessly, and you will die.

I felt so relieved and yet so guilty about Senenmut. How could I ever have thought him capable of treachery? And how was I now going to explain to him why he'd been kept out of this business, without revealing the true reason?

It was arranged that Kasmut would be escorted separately back to Thebes, while I returned to the palace with Hor and a contingent of the soldiers. The prisoners would come later under guard.

"In view of the seriousness of the situation, Your Highness," said Hor, "I'll send to the barracks for reinforcements. We mustn't underestimate Shushu's ability to be an awkward enemy, even now."

It was just bad luck I suppose, but what none of us had reckoned on was that the very first person we'd encounter at the gates of the palace would be – Shushu! I saw the look of alarm when he caught sight of us. As his eyes flickered from me, to Hor, to the group of soldiers and finally back to me again, it must have sunk in that he'd been rumbled. Then he did the unexpected thing. He turned and fled inside.

I don't blame them, but the soldiers were caught flat-footed, and Hor was slow to react too. Not me though. I didn't think about the consequences. I simply gave chase as if Shushu were Mek and I was still "Runner Girl". Behind me I heard Commander Hor's surprised bellow, "Follow her, men! Don't lose sight of them, whatever you do."

Shushu shot through the entrance hall, and then down the length of the palace rooms, heading for the harem, hoping perhaps to slow down his pursuers by going where permission was usually required to enter. He never once looked back. The women were startled to see us hurtle past in succession. I heard Nofret gasp and exclaim, "Asha, whatever's happening?" but I ignored her and ran on, followed at a distance by soldiers who were clearly in slightly worse physical shape than I was – at least when it came to a sprint.

Shushu took the route I would have chosen, bursting up the steps on to the first floor, along a corridor and then up a second, narrower flight on to the roofs. Then he was away towards the harem gatehouse, heading for the shops outside the palace, on the line of my old sky-skimming route. His stride was longer than mine, but it was still no problem to gain ground, although there was no point in catching him. What would I do if I did? He could easily overpower me. I immediately saw that my job was to maintain contact between Shushu and the soldiers. At all costs I had to keep the vizier in sight. Where the shops began he bounded down a staircase into the early morning bustle of the streets below, perhaps hoping to lose himself amongst people on their way to work. I tracked him along the street from the roofs, at one point beckoning the soldiers to split, some down to ground level and some to stay with me. As we went, I kept thinking to myself, *"What's in his mind? What would I do if I were him?"* Perhaps he was making for the river.

We careered on and on until, realizing there was a danger he'd lose us in a maze of passageways, I took some steps down into an alley. I had to hand it to Shushu. For a man of his age, not in regular exercise, he was doing very well. Even I was beginning to weary, but sheer panic carried him onwards. It was difficult down in the streets, avoiding people and stalls, but for a while I managed to keep him just in sight, before I let the soldiers clear a path through the crowds and take over the pursuit. After that I was a mere spectator to what followed.

I'll be brief. Shushu made it to the river in one piece. There was a papyrus skiff tied there. I never found out whether it belonged to him, or if he happened across it by pure chance. With only a few seconds to spare, he leapt aboard and precariously poled himself away from the small jetty just before the chasing soldiers could grab the end of the little boat. Standing up in its narrow stern, he wobbled out into the water between the reed beds. But clearly Shushu had been born to life as a courtier and not as a boatman. Not very far from the bank, his pole stuck fast. The skiff moved on, and the vizier, caught in two minds about whether to let go or twist it out, did neither and for a moment found himself suspended in mid-air before toppling into the water with a loud splash. He was unlucky. There was a sinister, violent thrashing in the reeds close by, as first one and then two giant crocodiles emerged to seize the helpless Shushu in their powerful jaws. We watched in awe as the mighty creatures threw him this way and that, repeatedly dragging him down beneath the muddied water, until he hadn't even the strength left to scream. Finally both human and crocodiles disappeared from view upstream amid the tangles of vegetation. Then there was only silence, apart from the sighing of the wind in the reeds.

Nothing of the vizier has ever been recovered, no limbs, no clothing. He has gone, as he deserved, to the great darkness, in utter disgrace.

Epilogue

Senenmut never fails to amaze me. His wisdom, his ability to read people, his knack of predicting what will happen. He was so gracious and understanding. "What else could you do?" he said. "You couldn't afford to trust anyone. I'd have advised you to act exactly as you did."

Everyone in court thinks him a fine vizier.

My mother Ahmose looks frail. It makes me cry when she says she hopes to rejoin hands with my father soon. As I look at her sad face, I think she's probably right and her time here is not long. I'll miss her as much as I miss him, but when the moment comes I shall be happy knowing they're together again.

A propitious day has been fixed for Nofret's marriage to Senbi in a month or so. They're in love, the way I'd always secretly hoped I would be, but know now I never will.

Rami comes to visit me, and when he does we talk for hours. I have endless excuses to see him, because I've commissioned his father Akhpet to design a grand series of artworks for the palace, including great statues of me and Edjmet, the twin Pharaohs.

Oh, I didn't tell you, did I? Edjmet has been increasingly poorly. Confidentially, the doctors tell me they think he may not live to the age of twenty summers. There are times when he can think clearly, and times when frankly he's a little mad. I take care of him as best I can, and soothe his fevered brow. I keep him as far away as I can from strong drink. It was my dear father's worst piece of judgement to allow Edjmet to succeed to the throne, and perhaps one of his best to make me marry him. As far as Egypt's concerned, that is.

And so with the approval of the chief priests, Senenmut, my mother, and the whole court, last month I was declared co-regent Pharaoh of Egypt alongside my husband. The Opet temple prophecy is coming true – a running girl is bringing prosperity at a time of difficulty. A young woman has proved to be the best man in the Two Kingdoms. I've been greatly honoured and blessed by Amun, and with his help I'll serve my country to make it a richer, more beautiful place. After which, when in turn I have journeyed to the next life, my unborn child will rule in my stead. And then, O goddess Nut, stretch thyself above me, and place me among the countless eternal stars which are in thee, that I may not die.

Historical note

By the time the Olympic Games come to London in 2012, it will be 1,600 years since Britain broke away from the Roman Empire. Asha's story is set 1,900 years before that, in what historians call the 18th Dynasty of Egyptian kings (a dynasty is a sort of family tree), so any Roman saying his or her final farewells to the white cliffs of Dover would think the life of Hatshepsut extremely ancient history. And one of the first ancient Egyptian kings, Narmer, lived at least 1,500 years before *that*!

Scholars divide Egyptian history into the Old Kingdom, the Middle Kingdom and the New Kingdom, each separated by Intermediate Periods when foreign invaders or local usurpers introduced new ideas and new ways of doing things. Even then historians add Early Dynastic and Late Periods at either end of the timeline to help us understand this enormous span of history. Queen Hatshepsut, the "Asha" of this book, lived early in the New Kingdom, perhaps 150 years or so before the famous Pharaoh Tutankhamun was born.

The sheer length of time ancient Egyptian civilization lasted, and its remoteness from us, are just two of the reasons why it's continued to fascinate people, particularly over the last 200 years. The French Emperor Napoleon was an early enthusiast. He commissioned an investigation into the intriguing remains his army "discovered" in the Egyptian desert and along the Nile.

At first sight it looks as if we know a huge amount about how ancient Egyptians lived and thought. Our libraries are full of books on many aspects of their lives, and if you want to find out more, you'll have no trouble doing so. Your computer will be a fantastic source of information too, but, for reasons I'll mention shortly, it needs to be used with care. But how do we know what we know?

Fortunately for us, the ancient Egyptians have handed down a lot of information on their lives by writing, carving and painting inscriptions on walls, papyri, and the potsherds and limestone flakes which archaeologists sometimes call ostraca. However, it was often the richer people who had access to these writing skills and who could afford the more expensive materials, so inevitably a great deal of what we know is about them rather than ordinary folk. And of course the 30 centuries of ancient Egyptian civilization mean customs, language and technologies may have changed a great deal over time. To take one example, how did the development of the wheel affect their civilization? (Somewhere just before the period in which this story is set, the ancient Egyptians learnt how to make war chariots, which helped them to remain the dominant military power.) We have to check our facts and not assume that what was true in the time of the famous Pharaoh Ramses II (circa 1250 BC) was for instance also true during the reign of King Khufu (circa 2550 BC).

Sometimes the surviving archaeology can mislead us too. We can still visit massive stone monuments and underground tombs (even though the grave-goods from these may have been robbed away), and learn a great deal about ancient Egyptian religion and funeral rituals from these marvellous public and private works. But the ordinary buildings, which housed, fed and entertained an estimated five million people at Egypt's peak of population, were made from mud-brick. This was a practical, plentiful material which was relatively easy to work, but in all except for a few cases it crumbled away long, long ago, taking priceless information about ordinary Egyptian lives with it.

So maybe now our ideas about the ancient Egyptians' attitudes to life, death and religion are skewed because of what we can still see. We have a similar problem when we try to interpret archaeology from periods in ancient British history. We marvel at great earthworks and tombs and we wonder at stone circles like the one at Avebury in Wiltshire. We can see where they sit in the landscape – often near to water – and we make quite reasonable guesses that religious rituals played a big part in the lives of our ancestors. After all, they (and the ancient Egyptians) lived short lives by comparison with our own, and had few effective remedies for serious illness or injury. Death and its meaning probably *was* an obsession for them. But we'll never know for certain whether this was more important to them than us.

The ancient Egyptians left us insights into their love lives, their sense of humour and their means of settling neighbourly disputes. We know how they organized their work. We catch glimpses of what the state required of the ordinary person in the way of service. We've been able to make sense of their written language, although we don't know what it sounded like. We can see what they wore, and we know some of the stories they liked to tell. We can look at pictures of their favourite musical instruments – and you may even catch a glimpse of a real one in a museum – but we don't know what their music was like to listen to. It all leaves lots of space for our imaginations to get to work.

In this book, the character of Hatshepsut is historical, although I don't know whether her friends really did shorten her name to Asha. I expect ancient Egyptians liked nicknames as much as we do, so it's possible! She was a great rarity – though not unique – a woman Pharaoh. But what do you make of the fact that some statues show her wearing a false beard? What difficulties did she have to overcome to convince her people that she was fit to rule? Senenmut was a real person too, and he *did* become her trusted and lifelong adviser, although I've invented the bit about him beginning his public life as her tutor. Hatshepsut's reign does seem to have brought prosperity to Egypt, but the chronology of when she married Thutmose II (to whom I've given the fictional first name Edjmet), whether they reigned together, whether she reigned on her own after his early death, or if she thereafter reigned together with her son Thutmose III isn't clear. Historians disagree about all this.

There's a mystery about what happened after Hatshepsut's death too. Many inscriptions about her were erased, as if some great disgrace became attached to her. Was it simply because she was a woman? It's one possibility, but we'll probably never know. Some people think that her mummified body, together with that of her nurse, Inet, survived and is now sitting in the museum in Cairo. At the time of writing scholars are arguing about which body is which, and whether either of them is authentic.

Thutmose I, his wife Ahmose and Asha's brother Wadjmose were all historical figures. The palace at Thebes and the harem certainly existed, but I've used my imagination as to what life might have felt like there and in the city. I made up the character of Shushu, although there would definitely have been a vizier, and the kind of ambitions Shushu harboured are quite believable. Of course, I completely invented the idea that Asha might have been into "free-running" as we now call it ("sky-skimming" in her words), and now I'm going to repeat a health warning. Please do not try this activity yourself on any account – roofs are dangerous places!

Egyptian civilization grew up because of peculiarities of the climate, the River Nile and the availability of natural resources. Is it a coincidence that the currently most complete account of early man's development (hundreds of thousands of years earlier) comes from fossils discovered in the vast area of Africa stretching down from Egypt through Ethiopia to present-day Kenya?

The Egyptians certainly passed on their engineering, mathematical and scientific skills to Greek, Roman, and Arab civilizations. It's probable that the ideas behind three major religions of our day – Judaism, Christianity and Islam – all owe something to Egyptian thought.

What you will certainly find, if you follow your nose along Web trails, is that the ancient Egyptians have also provided inspiration for a lot of – well, let's just call them "interesting" – theories about this and that. Some folk think that the pyramids are astronomical aids built with the help of aliens. Others are keen to explain that the ancient Egyptians travelled to South America and point to the existence of pyramid-like structures discovered on that continent as evidence. (The explorer Thor Heyerdahl believed he could demonstrate that reed boats were capable of crossing the Atlantic.) Others advance the idea that the Bible's Joseph

– the Technicolour Dreamcoat one – is the 4th Dynasty's historical character Imhotep. Mummies, tombs and curses have become regular "B" movie features. Ancient Egypt can become what you want it to be. So as Senenmut said to Asha *"Push your brain!"* And don't take anything on trust. Not even what you read in this book!

Timeline

These dates are approximate, and some of them are still the subject of debate!

circa 300,000 BC First known use of stone tools in what is now Egypt.

circa 7000-4000 BC Hunter-gatherers gradually turn to farming.

circa 3500 BC First walled towns in Egypt.

circa 3100 BC Egypt united under a single ruler.

circa 3000 BC 300 years after the Sumerians, the Egyptians develop writing.

circa 2680 BC The Old Kingdom. Pyramid-building begins.

circa 2500 BC (Stonehenge built in Britain.)

circa 2160 BC The First Intermediate Period.

circa 2040 BC The Middle Kingdom.

circa 1750 BC The Second Intermediate Period. First chariots.

circa 1550 BC The New Kingdom.

circa 1503 BC Hatshepsut born.

circa 1200 BC (The biblical Exodus from Egypt.)

circa 1100 BC (The Trojan wars.)

circa 1080 BC The Third Intermediate Period.

circa 710 BC Late Period.

circa 500–400 BC (The height of Ancient Greek civilization.)

332 BC Alexander the Great conquers Egypt.

30 BC Egypt becomes part of the Roman Empire.

AD 43 (Roman emperor Claudius invades Britain.)

AD 410 (The Roman Empire loses control of Britain.)

AD 1798 Emperor Napoleon begins his study of ancient Egypt.

AD 1853–1942 Sir Flinders Petrie: perhaps the greatest archaeologist of them all. He devoted much of his work to studying ancient Egypt.

Acknowledgements

A big thank you to Dr Kathryn Piquette, formerly of the Institute of Archaeology, University College London, for her many helpful comments, tactfully relayed, about the text of *Princess of Egypt*. Any historical inaccuracies are now the result of my obstinacy and not her scholarship.

And to Nahla, whose love of the country of her birth has been an inspiration, and who it turns out, was once a roof-runner too!

Picture acknowledgments

P 151	Alamy/Ian M Butterfield
P 152	The Art Archive/Egyptian Museum, Cairo Gianni Dagli Orti
P 152	Werner Forman Archive/British Museum, London
P 153	Alamy/David Paterson
P 153	Werner Forman Archive/E Strouhal
P 154	Werner Forman Archive/E Strouhal
P 155	Werner Forman Archive/E Strouhal
P 155	Alamy/Trip
P 156	Heritage-Images/Art Media
P 156	Heritage-Images/E&E Image Library

Statue of Hatshepsut from her temple at Deir el-Bahri.

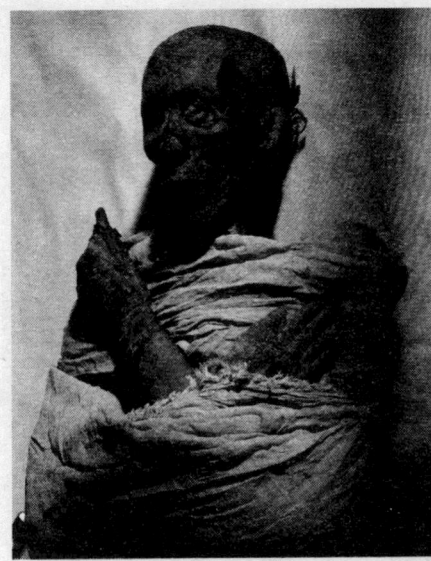

The mummy of Thutmose II. (Edjmet in this story!)

A wall-painting from the tomb of Nebamun, showing the nobleman hunting in the papyrus marshes near Thebes with his wife and daughter. Circa 1400 BC.

The temple at Karnak as it can be seen today.

A wall-painting from the tomb of the vizier Rekhmire showing
women playing music for a feast. Circa 1425 BC.

Looking across the River Nile from the east bank with the suburbs of Luxor to the right.

The horned goddess Hathor offers the sign of eternal life (an ankh) to Thutmose IV. From his tomb circa 1405 BC.

Women mourning. From the tomb of the vizier Ramose.

Ancient Egyptian model of a boat carrying a mummy to its tomb.

The great mortuary temple which Hatshepsut commissioned for herself (possibly from Senenmut) at Deir el-Bahri near Thebes.

Experience history first-hand with My Story –
a series of vividly imagined accounts of life in the past.

It's 1940 and with **London under fire**
Edie and her little brother are **evacuated**
to Wales. Miles from home and missing her family,
Edie is determined to be strong,
but when life in the countryside proves tougher than in
the capital she is **torn** between **obeying** her
parents and **protecting her brother...**

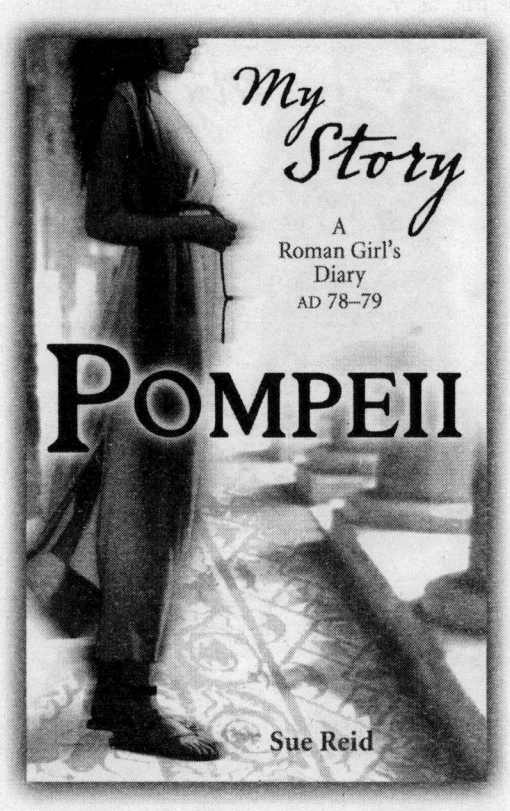

My Story

A
Roman Girl's
Diary
AD 78–79

POMPEII

Sue Reid

It's August AD 78 and Claudia is at
the Forum in Pompeii. It's a day of
strange encounters and even odder portents.
When the ground shakes Claudia is
convinced it is a bad omen. What does it all mean?
And why is she so disturbed by Vesuvius,
the great volcano that looms over the city...